THE MYTH OF
LOW SELF ESTEEM

A novel

Chana Studley

"I have been able to see so far by standing on the shoulders of giants"

Sir Isaac Newton

The Myth of Low Self Esteem

The Myth of Low Self-Esteem is a fictional memoir. I have tried to recreate events, locales, and conversations from my best memory of them. To maintain anonymity in some instances, I have changed the names of some of the individuals and places. The rest of the characters are fictional, and any resemblance to actual persons, living or dead, is purely coincidental. The information and opinions in this novel should not be regarded as a substitute for professional medical advice. The author can not be held responsible for any loss, claim or damage arising out of the misuse of the suggestions made or failure to take professional medical advice.

Cover design by Lauren Weinberg
Cover photos by Miryam Wasserman
Edited by Sarah Rosenbaum
Formatting by Rik – Wild Seas formatting

ISBN: 9781790894574

Chana Studley
www.chanastudley.com

Contents

1 Edgware   1
2 Manchester   5
3 London   24
4 Islington   37
5 Camden   41
6 Islington 2   48
7 Shoreditch   57
8 Leicester Square   70
9 North Hollywood   78
10 Sydney   85
11 Los Angeles   101
12 Pasadena   112
13 Santa Monica   120
14 Malibu   130
15 Universal Studios   134
16 Beverly Hills   139
17 Marina Del Rey   150
18 Austin and Chicago   163
19 El Segundo   172
20 San Francisco   185
21 Jerusalem   196
22 Tzfat   213
23 Tel Aviv   222
24 Venice Beach   227
25 New York   237
Acknowledgments   245
Bibliography   247
Resources   249

1
Edgware

It was September in a North London suburb, the first day of school not just for the children but for the school too. Somewhere in the middle of 300 wriggling and fidgeting children sat six-year-old Deborah, waiting patiently. All the children had been told to wait; some were managing and others, not so much. The building was brand new, squeaky-clean kind of new. Freshly painted and smelling of new carpet, optimism, and the favourite of teachers everywhere: Potential. No more 1940s' style wooden desks all in a row with an inkwell and a lid to bang up and down. No graffiti in the toilets or cigarette butts in the corners of the field and no gum under the chairs. It was all new. New books, new teachers, new everything.

The children were all eagerly waiting to hear which classroom they should go to.

"Kirsten Bechhofer... Tony Boyce..." read a teacher as she pointed to various places around the side of the bright, new auditorium.

"Ernest Berkhout...Tami Frank."

Another twenty children were called and got up to go to their places. Deborah started to get uncomfortable. She didn't mind the waiting, she was used to that — waiting for her brothers to play, waiting to be let down from the table, waiting, always waiting...but she was starting to get an uncomfortable feeling. She wondered who were going to be her new friends? Would the kids in her new class like her? What if her teacher didn't like her? She wasn't sure, but something didn't feel right.

"Joanna Fraser... Joanna, you forgot your bag! Miriam Frankel..."

Deborah felt nervous. She never liked going to new places. If she didn't know how it would be or how to do it, then she would rather not go, but there was no choice; she had to go to school. What if she made a mistake and the other kids laughed at her?

"Wendy Gorman..." called the teacher, pointing to a fourth-year group that was ready to leave for their classroom.

Half the children had left by now, and yet she was still sitting there in her tight pigtails and new cotton-print dress. School uniforms were a thing of the past apparently in this new, postmodern, open-plan '70s Junior School. It was a shoes off, sit on the carpet, and call your teacher Phil or Sue kind of school. Everything was new.

"Lee Hassel... Kayla Krieger..."

More kids had been chosen, and now Deborah was getting scared as she began to realise what was wrong. Maybe they had forgotten about her? What if she was supposed to be somewhere else? No, don't be silly...but then why wasn't her name being called... Maybe there was a letter, and her mum didn't get it? Perhaps they had read her name already, and she had missed it. Oh no! Should she stand up and tell the teacher? No, that might be a mistake and then she would be laughed at or told off. The thought of making a mistake and being laughed at was terrifying. Deborah was beginning to panic, just ever so slightly in her little six-year-old head. They don't know I'm here! I'm not on the list! They have forgotten about me!!

"Nicola McCormic... Micheal Peek... Nicholas Peters... Elisa Rubenstein."

By this time, there were only a handful of kids left sitting in the space that had opened up in the middle of the vast auditorium. The kids standing around the sides were staring at them with the kind of contempt reserved for the ones who never get picked for the team. It was crucifyingly painful. Deborah was dying of embarrassment. Her head was blowing a fuse, spraying sparks that she could feel coming into her eyes and out her of ears, her stomach was doing backflips. She knew they had forgotten about her, and her thoughts were raging with fear, shame, doubt, and back again. What would people think if her name wasn't on the list? Everyone would watch as she had to walk shamefully out of school and leave on her own. The feeling of being forgotten, unwanted, or not included was drilling its way through her little head and into her bloodstream.

"Becca Rome... Jonny Simmons... Deborah Stark..."

"...Deborah Stark!" repeated the teacher. Deborah was so wound up in emotional knots that she didn't or couldn't hear anything.

"DEBORAH RUTH STARK!"

Suddenly, in the middle of the hurricane that was raging in her head, she heard her name as the teacher came over to her and shouted it again. She was startled back to reality and stood to attention.

"Deborah Stark, go and stand with the other children in your class, you are holding everyone up!"

Now she really was embarrassed. Her face turned bright red, anger started to fill her chest, she felt like her head was going to explode. Why was she being blamed for keeping everyone waiting? It wasn't her fault they hadn't called her name earlier!

She hated the teacher, she hated the stupid

school, and she hated the other children for being chosen first. There were just two other kids left sitting on that newly polished auditorium floor that day out of 300.

Erika Windsor... and Lauren Weinberg

2
Manchester

1982

Manchester was the happening place to be in the early 1980s. The music scene and the people were the most compelling in the country, at least that's what it seemed like to eighteen-year-old Deborah and her new college friends who were drawn there. Deborah was an art student now, she had had a choice of either Camberwell School of Art and Design in London, Glasgow School of Art, or Manchester. London was too big and commercial, and Glasgow was just too far. Manchester, on the other hand, was bleak, rough, and Northern, which gave it a kind of dark honesty. It wasn't charming like Yorkshire, and well, it wasn't Liverpool. This all made it the best choice. It was the best city with the best music. Deborah was studying Embroidery at Manchester University by day and going to clubs and gigs by night. She always got a raised eyebrow when she told people she was doing a BA Honours degree in Embroidery. "Grannies do embroidery!" people would say to her, and not just because she was dressed all in black with her dreadlocks piled high up on her head.

"It should have been called, Fine Art Textiles," she told people, trying to explain what she was so excited to be studying. In her classes she was learning all there was to know about textiles and textile design. They learned print, knit, weave, and dyeing — even a stint in the fashion department. They had specialists come in to teach them ancient and modern skills like Victorian whitework, American Indian Beadwork, and millinery, and some very Marxist feminist art history teachers, who gave over their version of women's struggle for education, liberation, and freedom of expression. All this was going toward helping them develop their own style in textile art. Deborah's artwork was covered in charcoal and glue. Her teachers were puzzled by it, but encouraged her to keep exploring. It was a total indulgence of all her senses, and she soaked it up. The freedom that came with being away on her own was delicious. She could come home late, and no one was waiting up to give her a hard time. Deborah had escaped the tight, small world of her family down South, and could be herself without needing to make up stories about where she had been.

Manchester was cold and dismal, and she loved it. It wasn't called the rainy city for nothing. Apparently, it was something to do with the Pennines, but it always seemed to be raining. There were different kinds of rain, rain that came in sideways, rain that was so hard it bounced back up off the pavement, and sometimes you couldn't see that it was raining but would come home soaked through anyway. The old, filthy warehouses were still on Oxford Street, and the black industrial soot that clung to the statues and spires was perfect. The grunge of post-industrial Manchester suited the music, the politics, and her very cynical outlook on life. She had already seen the best bands — The Slits, Joy Division, The Pop Group — and quickly found new friends with the same abstract look at life at the Student Union bar on Oxford Street. They were the cool, post-punk, alternative crowd, some of whom were still going to class and some who were just pretending. She had escaped home on the pretence of education and soon found other students who had done the same. For many of them, class was a necessary inconvenience between the bar at lunchtime and clubs at night. Kirsten was from Edinburgh, Harry was from somewhere posh down South, and Dave the DJ was from Birmingham. Mick was from Crawley, south of London, and was joined later by his friends Roma and Steve, who had finished with college somewhere else up North. The music scene in Manchester in the late Seventies and early Eighties was the best in the country. There was always a band to see or a nightclub opening up, places to be seen and to see who else was being seen.

Everyone was in a band. Everyone's lives revolved around music, the latest records from the latest alternative bands. Harry was in a band that was doing really well, and Chris, a History student in his last year, was their manager. They had just come back from a Scandinavian tour, and the Chernobyl atomic reactor had exploded while they were gone, so Deborah had put their postcard in a plastic bag, you know, just to be on the safe side. Excited to see them, she and Kirsten piled down to some dark nightclub on Ancoats to hear them play. The crowd was a heaving mass of spikey hair and attitude with only the lights from the stage to flash any illumination on the dance floor. She and her friends lost themselves as they danced in the dark to the grungy rhythms of the music.

In between the flashing lights, Deborah became aware of a young man who was trying to dance with her. He was wearing a leather jacket, not a biker one, but a sleazy 80s' suit style one. She didn't know him, never saw his face, but she felt him put his hands where he shouldn't. Annoyed, she started shouting above the noise for him to back off, but he didn't. He kept trying to dance with her and when she resisted he began to pull her off to the side. She kept yelling at him to stop. No one heard her cries for help above the noise. She felt that same panic as when she was six years old, forgotten and alone in the crowd. Kirsten and Roma didn't hear either, and she didn't know where Mick or Steve were. As she tried to push him away and get to the safety of her friends, she suddenly felt his hand on the back of her head, and with great force, he smashed her head down into a concrete pillar on the side of the dance floor!

Everything went black. Deborah only lost consciousness for a few seconds, but as she came to, she could sense her forehead was a different shape! Alarmed, she realized it wasn't just dark because her face was suddenly on the floor. She had almost lost her eyesight and could only see about an inch in front of her nose! She was scared, something was terribly wrong, and she knew she had to get help. Dazed and half-blind, she crawled on her hands and knees through the crowd to the back of the room where she knew Chris was working the sound system. With all her strength, she pulled herself up and slumped over the mixing desk. As soon as he saw her, Chris leapt over the bar and grabbed a bucket of ice, poured it into a bar towel for her head, grabbed Kirsten, and they all bundled into a taxi to the hospital. Deborah was conscious but totally panicked; she didn't know what was happening or where she was. At the hospital she flailed around trying to make sense of it all, still unable to see more than a few inches, she lashed out whenever anyone tried to come near her head. Grabbing hold of Kirsten for safety and pushing away the nurses who were trying to take the clips out of her hair for the X-ray, Deborah continued to struggle, feeling like she was still being attacked. The confusion, the noises, the darkness were terrifying. The nurses had to get an X-ray, and so they had no choice but to put her in four-point restraints to stop her from falling off the table and hurting herself again. She couldn't see Chris's or Kirsten's face, but she could sense that they were scared too. Finally, they were able to calm her down, and everyone left the X-ray room while she lay there alone and frightened under the fluorescent lights in the cold stainless steel of the emergency room. Two hours later, at 3 a.m., they were told that Deborah's skull had been fractured, and she was sent home with a sick note to miss class for the rest of the week.

She came to early the next morning and found Harry asleep on her sofa. He had stayed to make sure she was okay but was out cold after a month of touring and his gig the night before. She struggled to remember what had happened. Her eyesight had mostly returned, but she could sense the swelling on her forehead was gruesome. As she lay in bed, she gently ran her fingers over the tight, tender skin. There was no cut. There wasn't even much pain, just this fuzzy, spaced-out feeling and a vague sense of dread. Deborah could just about remember the doctor asking her to follow his finger, to which she had replied, *Which one?* Suddenly, she was throwing up in the bathroom. She slumped back into bed, feeling awful. Harry still hadn't stirred. Deborah was wondering what to do next when she noticed a small card from the hospital by her bed. It was a warning about the signs of brain damage following a head injury, one of which was vomiting.

For the next few days she stayed on the sofa, Kirsten brought her cups of tea, and Mick and Steve affectionately called her Melon Head. Slowly the swelling started to go down, and she began to feel normal again. It didn't occur to her to go back to the hospital or the doctor. Her mother had been a children's nurse, so she had grown up in a home where you only went to the emergency room if your arm was hanging off or you were dying. It wasn't right to waste the doctor's time with silliness when they had really sick people to deal with. So she and her sore head spent an unexpected week off, nursed by good friends with tea and sympathy.

As one of her visitors sat drinking tea, admiring the now many shades of green and purple that had stealthily made their way across Deborah's swollen forehead like an advancing army, Kirsten retold the dramatic story of how Deborah had fallen, and they had all rushed off to the hospital in the taxi.

"I didn't fall," said Deborah.

"Yes, you did," corrected Kirsten, patting her compassionately and looking at her like maybe she had brain damage after all...

"No, he attacked me!"

"Who did?"

"I don't know! He wanted to dance with me, and I pushed him away, next thing I knew his hand was on the back of my head slamming it down into concrete!"

Her friends sat staring at her, stunned into silence.

As the week went by, Deborah recovered and went back to college and music and concerts and the life of a student. Thank God the only long-term problems were that her handwriting was never the same again and for about the next ten years after the injury, she would have what she called verbal dyslexia. At random moments, words would just come out in the wrong order. It was quite embarrassing at times. She would be saying something quite intelligent, then suddenly she would be speaking gobbledygook.

After leaving college, Deborah stayed in Manchester for a few years, and things were pretty good. She worked in the trendy vegetarian Greenhouse restaurant in the evenings, which was a great way to earn money while hanging out with her friends who either worked there or came to eat. All the local hipsters would come to the Greenhouse for the food and the scene, like trendies from the BBC and, of course, Manchester's most famous vegetarian, Morrissey, who would come in for his mint tea and apple crumble and sit facing the corner, not talking to anyone. She did a few freelance artistic jobs around the city and started thinking about what she would do next.

During college Deborah had been living in Hulme, a 1960s disaster of modern architecture that the city council had deemed unsuitable for families and was now a ghetto for punks, students, and packs of roaming dogs. Everyone was on the Dole, the Miners were on strike, and effigies of Mrs. Thatcher were being burnt on Bonfire Night instead of Guy Fawkes. If you could get to the post office to cash your unemployment check without being bitten by one of the stray dogs, you were having a good day! The families that had previously been kicked out of their "2 up 2 down" pre-war, little red-brick houses due to no indoor plumbing had now been kicked out of this maze of concrete flats, with its skywalks and colour-coded doors, asbestos, and high suicide rate. Deborah had grown up in an England where everything was either before the war or after the war. These dreary post-war concrete blocks of flats had each been named after great British architects, and everyone was sure that Charles Barry, John Nash, and William Kent must have been turning in their graves at this travesty of design that carried their names.

It was time for Deborah to move on, and so she had just moved out of Hulme to an attic flat in a grand, old Victorian house in Victoria Park on the other side of the city center. It had character and elegance; the big, heavy, white front door was inlaid with black designs; there was even a statue above the entrance. The floor-to-ceiling sash windows looked out over a garden, and the communal hall and stairs were decorated in deep, Indian-restaurant flocked wallpaper and carpet. It had magnificence and charm compared to the house she had grown up in, which was painfully average. The painting above her parents' never-used fireplace was a print from a department store to match the sofa set. Everything was in its place, and nothing was ever moved. Deborah had been shocked the first time she visited the home of a teenage friend to see real art on the wall, the kind where you could see actual brush strokes in the thickness of the paint, and there were books on the stairs! At home, books only went on bookshelves, and the only thing allowed to stay on the stairs was the Axminster carpet. The most exotic thing in their house was a piece of wood supposedly from the Mount of Olives with the word *Shalom* in very ugly 1970s' greenish-yellow Hebrew that her parents had picked up on a package tour to Israel.

The day after the move, she had arranged with her old neighbour Dil to pick up a few last things she had left with him. Dil's parents were Tolkien fans and had named him Elendil after a character in Lord of the Rings. An architecture student by day and a drummer at night, it was kind of ironic for him to be living in William Kent Crescent. She had walked this route so many times. It was the way to the Moss Side shopping center and the stinky launderette that everyone from that side of Hulme used. At 6 p.m. in February, Manchester is already dark and misty, so she walked briskly between the two housing estates along a small side road next to a piece of waste ground, eager to get to Dil's and warm herself up by his two-bar electric fire. She was musing about her new flat and about which pictures she would put up where, when suddenly, out of the dark, she heard footsteps come up fast behind her. In that split second, she knew she was in danger, and there was nowhere to turn. Three young men came running out of the dark and jumped her from behind dragging her to the ground. It was so fast and furious, she couldn't do anything to stop them. Deborah struggled and screamed for her life as they punched and kicked her in the head and the chest and stomach. It must have only lasted a few minutes, but it was long enough to fill her with absolute terror. They punched and kicked her repeatedly, trying to get to her pockets. She fought back, but by now they had her arms pinned down, the only thing she could do was scream for her life. In the middle of this terrifying chaos, she had a bizarre sensation. She could hear herself screaming as if she was watching from above. It was as if she was watching from about twenty feet up, looking down. Yet at the same time, she could feel the air running out of her lungs. She could feel gut-wrenching panic filling up the rest of her body as the last few drops of air left her chest. She knew that if she couldn't catch another breath, she was going to die. She knew that if they had a knife it was over and she was going to die. She couldn't see their faces, they had hoods up, and in the chaos and darkness, all she could make out was that there were three of them: one on each side, and the other trying to hold her down. Realising she had nothing for them to steal, they left as suddenly as they had arrived, leaving Deborah concussed, cut and bruised, crumpled up in the dirt on the side of the road like a used rag. Very slowly and still half-dazed, she managed to pull herself up onto her elbows and, to her horror, she could see a man in a raincoat walking by on the other side of the piece of ground where she lay! It was dark, but she could see him clearly in the damp air under the streetlamp, and yet another person ahead of him, disappearing into the night. She had been screaming for her life, and they had kept walking?! Abandoned and alone, Deborah struggled to get herself up and stumbled her way to Dil's flat. Dil did his best to take care of her wounds, gave her cups of tea, and then helped her get a taxi home.

Nobody knew the words 'post-traumatic stress disorder' back then, or if they did, no one in Manchester told Deborah about it. Instead, she shut herself up in her flat for a few days to nurse her wounds. The cuts and bruises were painful, her head throbbed, and it was hard to stand up straight, as her stomach muscles were so sore. Maybe there was a broken rib or two, so she just lay still. After a few days had passed, she needed some food, so she got herself up and dressed to go to the local shop. As she hobbled down the stairs and slowly approached the front door, she heard a thought pass through her mind. It said, *Last time you went out this door, they almost killed you!* She stopped, she felt panicked, her body tightened, and she started to breathe very quickly. Outside it was a crisp winter afternoon, the sky was pale grey, and the bare trees stood still in the faint sunlight. As she walked carefully across the damp garden and down the road, through an alley and across the main road to the local shop, she was painfully aware of everything, her eyes darting everywhere to see what or who was near her. By the time she made it home, she was exhausted, shaking, and very confused.

The next day Deborah decided that the police should know what happened. Her distress and confusion were giving way to turmoil and anger as she thought about how she had not done anything to deserve what had happened, so she started to venture out to the Police station to give them a report. As she approached the front door, there was a bitter taste in her mouth, her heart started to beat faster as she heard that same thought say, *A few days ago you went out this door, and they almost killed you.* Only this time it reminded her that no one had come to her aid. The tight jaw and stomach-wrenching panic were there again, and her breathing was rapid. Deborah walked quickly, straight to the police station, watching everyone and everything with desperate vigilance. If anyone came near her or moved too suddenly, she gasped and stepped back, rigid with fear. At the police station, she was invited into a dark interview room and asked to sit down. A young detective with reddish hair and sallow skin wrote down all her details and then, without looking up and with all the emotion of a wet fish, said, "We know who did it."

Deborah stiffened.

"Yeah," he continued, "these guys have been attacking women in this area for a while now."

She wanted to reach across the table grab and him by the throat! "Why aren't you doing anything about it?"

"Oh... 'Cause we have real things to deal with, Luv." and he went back to his paperwork.

Deborah didn't go out for a few days after that. Her thinking was starting to turn on her. It kept reminding her that no one had stopped to help and that the police didn't even think she was worth bothering with. Her friends were great at the beginning, Kirsten had come several times to make her tea, Dil had called to check on her, and Roma covered her shifts at the restaurant. But now that the cuts and bruises were healing, they had moved on to the next drama. And besides, she was in a different neighborhood now, so she knew she had to cope on her own. Her thoughts became her companions, talking to her all day and all night, reliving the attack and telling the story over and over, recounting every detail that happened as if this time she would really be able to explain the depths of terror she was still feeling.

Deborah decided to take some time off from working at the restaurant. She knew that dealing with people and their stupid questions about the menu was just too much for her, but soon she needed to go out again for food. As she started to move to the front door, the thoughts about the attack started up again. *Ten days ago when you went out this door, they nearly killed you!* The voice in her head had moved in and was taking up all the spare room with its constant commentary, like a roommate who won't shut up and talks all the way through your favourite TV show. Two weeks went by and she was getting a little crazy with it. She couldn't stop reliving what had happened, and any time she would think about going out, panic would take over, and she couldn't think straight. *Three Tuesdays ago, you went out, and you were attacked! Four Tuesdays ago, you went out, and they almost killed you!*

This continued for months, and Deborah became quite frantic and frail. She was completely distracted and felt isolated and helpless. She spent her days looking out the window, watching the people going by getting on with their lives, and wondered how they did it. She just couldn't keep her relentless thoughts straight, and she couldn't concentrate on anything. She had always had some kind of art project going, like the handmade quilt she had been working on for months. She got it out to work on but just couldn't see the point of it anymore. Everything seemed like such hard work, and for what? She just couldn't remember. There was no cable TV or computers to fill up the time, and getting to the video store was like an expedition to

Mars. So she found herself staring at the wall or out the window for hours. Life was becoming a living nightmare. She remembered a scene from one of her favourite movies, *Breakfast at Tiffany's*. The heroine, played by Audrey Hepburn, says, "The Blues are when you get fat and it rains too much. You're just sad, that's all. The Mean Reds are horrible, suddenly you are afraid and you don't know why... Well, when I get the Mean Reds, the only thing that works is to jump in a cab and go to Tiffany's...nothing bad can happen to you there...if only I could find a real, live place like Tiffany's, I'd move in and give the cat a name!" Deborah stared out the window at the grey Manchester rain. There was no cat and no Tiffany's.

Deborah would talk to her friends on the phone but didn't really tell them what was going on. She didn't understand it herself, so how could she explain it to anyone else? How could she tell anyone how she spent her time: scared of every little thing, anxious and angry, crying herself into exhaustion night after night? Soon she was living in a kind of twilight world of before the attack and after the attack, and now her thinking was attacking her! At best it was reliving the attack, and at worst, it told her no one cared, and life was not worth living. She couldn't sleep because the nightmares were too terrifying and she wasn't eating properly, partly because getting to the shop was too stressful, and even if she tried to eat, the food just wouldn't get past her throat. She could be starving, faint with hunger, and would have to spit out the food, it just wouldn't go down. It was as if her throat was closed and she couldn't swallow a thing. She was becoming quite strange. She found herself in the middle of obsessive rituals that somehow gave her a sense of control in her out-of-control world. She would make sure the radio or TV were on when she picked up the phone so that she seemed like a normal, busy person though she knew she wasn't. She literally felt like she was suffocating, struggling at times to breathe, the panic was so severe. Her head was swirling with flashbacks and confusion as to how this could have happened to her. She felt like she was paddling frantically in the sea trying to keep her head above the waves, always fearful that she could be sucked under at any moment. Her sadness was slowly drowning her as each hour passed.

Spring had passed her by and then, one summer morning, as she slowly opened her eyes, she could feel intense pain in her hand. She looked down to see it was swollen and bruised! How did that happen? She wondered. Slowly, very slowly, she remembered in a very dark moment of absolute frustration and despair she had punched the wall the night before! She panicked! Was she going mad? She felt helpless like she had slipped into some kind of living nightmare, a horror movie that wouldn't end. A few days later she was woken again by the throbbing of a swollen and bruised hand. It became a routine, hurting her precious hands and then hiding them, scared someone would see but desperate for someone to notice. By the end of the summer, exhausted by this secret existence, Deborah forced herself to go back to work at the Greenhouse Restaurant. She knew she had to get out and try to get back to a normal life, and doing something productive seemed like a good idea. But it was an act. She made up some lie about the bruises and did a good job of pulling it off, but the burden of carrying around this big secret, the secret life of a mad woman, the dark and terrifying thoughts that were continually screaming in her head, was taking its toll. Her verbal dyslexia was made worse by this new stress, so waiting tables was just too frightening. Many times when the customers would ask for the specials or want to book a large reservation, she would get her words muddled up, and the looks of disgust and pity were unbearable. Hiding out in the security of the kitchen with Kirsten, preparing the food, was much safer. Deborah's body wasn't functioning properly by now, so she finally went to see her doctor, and somehow he picked up on what was happening. She didn't remember telling him anything about the attack, but a week later, a letter came from the Manchester Royal Infirmary Psychiatric Unit. Deborah stood in the hallway of her big, old house reading the letter. She couldn't believe it, she was being summoned to see a psychiatrist, and if she didn't go, they would come and get her! She had only ever known one person who had gone to a psychiatrist, a kid from her secondary school who had tried to kill himself, but she wasn't like that. She knew things weren't right but this was all a big mistake, she could pull herself out of it if she wanted to. British people just didn't go to psychiatrists unless they needed to be locked up, and therapy was something that Americans did. Holding the letter in her hand kind of made it a bit too real. She felt cornered as if someone had been watching her; was someone spying on her?

She went.

Manchester Royal Infirmary psychiatric unit was in the beautiful, original, old red-brick hospital building with its Gothic 19th-Century facade and long, ghostly corridors. It smelt of chlorine. The walls had been painted over and over, and the polished floors made the nurses' shoes squeak as they walked busily up and down. There were still a few things left from the 1950s, like the green canvas-and-metal hospital screens and the standard green china tea service seen in all good British Institutions after the war. She sat in the waiting room with several other people who were clearly mad. One was banging his head against the wall and the other, a young girl, was drooling. Deborah looked away, scared she would heave, it was so disgusting. How did she get here?! She couldn't process what was happening. This was clearly a mistake, she wasn't that kind of crazy. As her thoughts started to run faster and faster circles around the inside of her head, the now familiar voice was whispering to her that she should get up and leave, that this was all a big misunderstanding, and that she should just get up now quickly before they could find out what was really happening and have her locked up.

"Deborah Stark?" called the nurse, Deborah got up and went in. The psychiatrist was a young blonde, not much older than herself, and looked like she knew nothing about the real world. The walls of her office had been painted over and over too. The current coat of paint was light blue. There were toys in the corner for kids, and pictures of green fields and snowy mountains Blu-tacked to the walls in a lame attempt to be calming. One wall was all windows overlooking a courtyard where people in pajamas and bathrobes were doing the lithium shuffle, supervised by hospital orderlies.

The doctor sat at her desk, looked over some paperwork, and then asked about the attack. Deborah answered her questions, and then the psychiatrist asked her how she felt about the attack. Deborah just looked at her resisting the temptation to be sarcastic. She wanted to scream, *How do you think I feel?! I feel bloody terrified! I wouldn't be here if I didn't!* But she was too well brought up to be rude to a doctor and just shrugged her shoulders. The psychiatrist asked her to describe it again and how she felt about it. Deborah got frustrated. She couldn't understand why the doctor wanted her to keep going back over what happened, she could do that quite well on her own at home. She needed help with how not to do that! *Stupid cow*, thought Deborah. It seemed so pointless. It took so much effort to get there, all those roads and people to negotiate, and a full-on panic attack trying to find the right department — and for what? It made no sense. Deborah sensed threat and danger everywhere and retelling it to the psychiatrist just added to the panic and pain in her head. She had had enough of that already. Deborah couldn't or wouldn't tell her about how she was living now. Why should she trust this stupid woman with her very private nightmare when she clearly didn't have a clue how to help? She left the session feeling just as bad, if not worse, than when she arrived, and after three visits of the same stupid questions, she swore never to go back.

Out in the backyard of the restaurant, there was a large chest freezer covered with a massive wooden case to protect it from the harsh Manchester winters. One sunny September afternoon about eight months after the attack, as she was setting up for the evening shift, she lifted the heavy wooden lid to hook it onto the wall so that she could open the freezer and get out some mushroom strudel and nut roast for the evening crowd. Very quietly, the familiar voice whispered its way through her head. It was such an innocent, quiet thought, the kind that you could almost not notice, like, *Hmmm, what shall I have for dinner, mushroom strudel or the fresh vegetable curry?* It had an almost friendly, familiar voice by now, like a roommate just saying "bye" as they popped out to do an errand. It said, *Put your hand here and let go of the lid.* She gasped, "OH MY..." Adrenaline shot through her from her head to her toes. She woke up. It shook her to the core, not just because her hand would have been smashed to pieces but how natural and friendly this deadly thought was.

That night, Deborah sat on the edge of her bed. She felt like her life was out of control, she felt like a lemming running toward the edge of a cliff, only she was the one saying, "Throw yourself off"! She sat upright and rigid and tried to think it through. Her thinking had gotten the better of her, so she had to stop it, or she could see that sooner or later someone was going to have to stop it for her. This was critical. It was life or death, and she had to think hard. Trying to think clearly from such a dark place was like ploughing through thick mud, like someone who had been paralysed struggling to walk again. She felt like she had no choice but to come up with a plan.

She wasn't sure where it came from, but the plan was simple. Every time she would catch herself thinking destructive thoughts or reliving the attack, she would tell herself to shut up. That was it, just Shut Up. The problem was that her thinking was so contaminated that she was going to have to yell at herself to shut up all the time! When she was on her own, she would shout it out loud, and if she had made it out of the flat, she would scream it in her head. "SHUT UP, SHUT UP, SHUT UP!" She had a feeling the psychiatrist probably wouldn't approve, but it was all she could think to do. Deborah's pride conspired with her mind not to tell anyone what she was doing. In her secret, crazy little messed up world, she was fighting for her life.

"SHUT UP, SHUT UP, SHUT UP!" Deborah didn't know how long it continued, but strangely, it began to work. After maybe a few months of policing her thoughts and bringing in a big stick to smash them, she managed to get at least the constant daily reliving of the attack to quiet down a little. Like naughty school children, the thoughts were beaten into submission and only popped up when she wasn't watching. She knew this was crazy, but she was a crazy person who wanted desperately to survive. It was hard work, but Deborah felt she had no choice.

It was the end of January. The days were short, and the sky and the trees were bare again, and everything reminded Deborah that it was coming up to a year since the attack. As her thoughts began gearing up for a grand anniversary pity party, she finally realized what the problem was. She had a massive revelation, or was it a profound insight? The problem was clearly Manchester, and the solution was to move to London.

3
London

By her mid-twenties, Deborah had discovered that she could make pretty much anything with her hands. She had spent hours as a child making dolls' houses, gifts, and games out of cereal boxes and sticky-backed plastic, lollipop sticks and paper mache. She would lose herself in little worlds created inside shoe boxes with tiny curtains at tiny windows and tiny little people made from pipe cleaners and beads. Her dream was to one day make the magical scenes that were displayed in the Department store windows at Holiday time, but creating miniature worlds in shoe boxes, where everything was safe and quiet, kept her happy as a child. Hours glued to the BBC children's television show *Blue Peter* had prepared her perfectly for a career in making something out of the things she found lying around the house or in the garden shed. Her mother sewed, and her father had built their first Hi-Fi out of a Heathkit, soldering the transistors and making the speaker cabinets himself. He and her two older brothers had created a whole model railway world in the attic, complete with paper mache hills, tunnels, and signal boxes. They had their fantasy world up in the roof, but Deborah was too little to climb the ladder safely, so she made her own fantasy world down in her room. Her time in the Textiles Department at University had taught her how to use almost anything to create, and solve problems when other people didn't know where to start. Her hands could move from a fine silk thread to a power drill to a paintbrush and back again to produce exactly what you wanted, so she began to look for work with anyone who would pay her to make things. Jobs like these were never advertised, it was that spooky thing of "who you know" more than what you know, and being in the right place at the right time.

Shortly after arriving in London she got up the courage to walk into her local Community Arts Theater. *You can do this,* whispered Deborah under her breath after yelling at herself to shut up all morning. The Oval House Theater was just south of the river near the top of Brixton Road where she had found a small flat. It was the kind of place that did experimental theater, with a vegan cafe and signing for the deaf. She looked around and offered to help with the costumes and props for their next production. It was something minimalistically weird, but this introduced her to a whole new world of artists and designers who introduced her to even more. Before long her career took off, and she was designing and making things for an array of creative people and situations. From floats and costumes for the Notting Hill Carnival to world tour sets for the Rolling Stones and Tina Turner. She even spent one summer revamping all the furniture for the Royal Opera House at their warehouse down by the river. Before long there were projects at the Tower of London, The Imperial War Museum, she was even flown up to Scotland to help build a private museum for Cutty Sark Whiskey at their distillery out in the middle of the Highlands. She worked on costumes for Les Miserables that were sent to Broadway in New York, headdresses for the Royal Shakespeare Company, and even designed the holiday decorations for Covent

Garden and Oxford Street for the millions of London tourists and shoppers to enjoy. And finally, her childhood dream came true when she was asked to design and make decorations to go in the windows at Harrods and Tiffany's in Knightsbridge! After just a few years Deborah was living the dream, she had made a name for herself and was in demand. Creative directors knew they could tell her whatever crazy thing they needed and she would make it for them, sometimes in cavernous warehouses that had been there since before Charles Dickens' time and sometimes on her bedroom floor. If you looked at her resume, things were going very well; she had the Thought Police employed full-time, and her thinking was under control. Working all the hours God sent helped to keep the dark thoughts locked away and her mind out of trouble. Thinking positive and keeping busy, that was the answer.

Some really fascinating people moved through the doors of The Oval House Theater, like Eugene, the son of a Zulu Chief who had been Steve Biko's getaway driver in the fight against apartheid in South Africa. His wife, Miriam, had been imprisoned for giving birth to their first child. Having a black baby in South Africa, for a white woman in the late 80s, was a criminal offence. As soon as they had been released from prison, the family had fled to London as political refugees. Deborah reveled in this new exciting world of creativity and politics. There was always a party to go to or a gallery opening with London's alternative, artsy crowd and free tickets to shows. Something intriguing was always happening.

Deborah had bought herself a mountain bike, it was the latest thing at the time for exercise and getting around. As she rode home from helping Eugene plaster the walls of his new but broken-down home found for him by Amnesty International, she noticed out of the corner of her eye a 16-year-old boy on a little kid's bike. As she passed him she thought to herself it was a bit strange; the bike was way too small for him, he looked like he had stumbled out of Lilliput! It was about 10 p.m. and she was peddling fast, it had been a long day of physically hard work at the theater since 7 a.m. and then plastering at Eugene's till late. Suddenly the boy was off the bike and had swung it around at her head! Before she knew it, she was in the gutter, cars whizzing past just inches from her nose as he snatched her mountain bike out from under her and was gone into the night! The impact was ferocious, like being shot out of a cannon at a brick wall and over in seconds. As she lay there, face down in the oily, wet dirt of a London street gutter unable to move, she screamed inside her head, *Why me?...... WHY ME? I don't understand it, why do all these things keep happening to me?!* Dazed and confused she stumbled back to Eugene's house, where Miriam held her as she sobbed uncontrollably.

The next day Deborah had an interview for a real job at the BBC props department, and nothing was going to stop her from showing up, she had worked so hard for this opportunity. Fueled by adrenaline and a lot of coffee, she was determined to go. Somehow, with a stabbing pain in her neck and a weird sensation in her body, she managed to get herself to Waterloo Station to catch the train out to Teddington Lock. Shaking and stumbling, she made it through the interview, and then trying her best to walk normally she cautiously followed the BBC prop manager as he showed her around a new TV show that was being filmed called, *Absolutely Fabulous*. She felt absolutely terrible as she made her way back to Waterloo, then right there under the big Victorian station clock, she collapsed. Several people came to help her to a seat where she sat shaking in the middle of hundreds of busy Londoners and commuters dashing in all directions.

The next morning Deborah slowly opened her eyes... She was home, but something was very wrong. She was utterly unable to lift her head off the pillow! She rolled over but still could not sit up. She tried not to panic. Supporting her head with both hands, Deborah slid off her bed and very slowly made it to the bathroom to look in the mirror. She looked normal, no bruises or swelling but there was no strength in her neck, it was limp like a ragdoll. She flopped back to bed and stayed there till the next day when she felt brave enough to get to the doctor. Deborah's doctor moved her head around and said she was fine and sent her home. But she wasn't fine, far from it.

Later that night Miriam came to visit with some disturbing news. Her daughter had overheard a kid in her class bragging about how he had stolen a bike while the girl was still on it and when the boy realized they knew who he was, he had come to their house and set the dustbins on fire! Eugene and Miriam had four small children by now, and they were scared.

"You have to go to the police, Deborah. This is too dangerous! Who knows what he might do next time!"

Deborah couldn't comprehend the thought of going to the police again after the way she was treated last time. She hated that detective, her blood started to move faster as she thought about him.

"Please Deborah, I'll go with you. I'll pick you up tomorrow?" pleaded Miriam. "Please, for my kids' sake?"

Deborah resisted. It wasn't just the thought of talking to the Police that distressed her. She knew that once this kid was sucked into the System, his life would be over and she didn't want to be responsible for that. Miriam continued to plead with her and finally, she gave in and found herself back in a police interview room giving details of another violent attack. Two days later, she heard from Eugene that the boy had been picked up for stealing cars.

Deborah's neck was still very weak and painful, she had to support her head as she moved around, it was just too weak to hold up by itself. Stumbling around, she found a medical supply place and bought herself one of those big neck collars, the type you see in movies about American lawyers and car accidents. She felt vulnerable and scared and needed something to give her a sense of protection. Deborah found herself sitting in her flat staring into space. She felt alone, her body tensing with every hour that passed, and her thinking started to turn dark again. She knew the signs, the quiet whispering voice reliving the event over and over, the raging anger and helplessness, and her magical hands that gave her and others such joy with their creativity were clenched again. This time it happened fast, the Thought Police were AWOL. Her thinking was attacking her from all angles day and night, she didn't want to talk to anyone, her neck was killing her, and she was exhausted. Deborah felt as if she was looking down a very dark well. Despair was creeping in, and everything felt so very heavy. "Shut up, shut up," she told herself, but she didn't have the energy to fight anymore. Every time she had pulled herself together, she just got hit again, and she started to ask herself, what was the point. Either life, God, whatever you wanted to call it, was out to get her, or was there just some grand conspiracy against her? She began to lose all touch with reality; she wasn't eating, couldn't sleep at night, and couldn't stay awake during the day. The world made no sense to her, and the rage in her head was loud. Night and day, day and night, her thinking was in what felt like that last spin cycle in an industrial washing machine. She knew by now without any doubt that if she left her flat, a bus was going to lose control and run her over. She was terrified of even the thought of going down into an Underground Station for fear someone would push her in front of a train! Deborah was convinced that some kind of Murphy's Law was at work and it was on a special mission to get her. She knew it was true, she had evidence: three times she had been beaten down, and each time she got up, she got beat down again. No one could blame her if she gave up, she was innocent, life was out to get her, and she didn't understand why.

Deborah spent hours crying, throwing things at the wall, raging, sobbing on the bathroom floor, tormented by her thoughts. Was it some sick joke? It was dark outside, was it 6 a.m. or 6 p.m.? She couldn't tell anymore. She was so tired. Should she just give up and drown in misery and despair in a lunatic asylum somewhere? Was there a point to any of it? For days she lived in limbo, losing all sense of time and normality, stumbling around her flat not knowing what to do and then collapsing again, choking in floods of desperate tears on the floor. She would get up and then fall back down again. This seemed to be all life was, one big slap in the face after another. It felt like her world had closed in to about two feet around her, she was pinned up against her bedroom wall frozen in fear and then...just like that ......it stopped.

The hurricane stopped.

There was...... Quiet.

It was as if someone had just flipped a switch. All the raging and the catastrophic noise of constant screaming in her head just...... stopped, like someone had pressed a mute button.

Afraid to turn her head or move even an inch, her eyes scoured the room. Nothing had changed. Nobody was there except the Quiet. Slowly she pulled herself together, washed her face and sat with this new visitor, Quiet, and the Quiet sat with her. They sat together on her bed, cautious of each other. She was suspicious. Where had this Quiet come from, what did it want? What did it mean?

Deborah felt uneasy, a little nervous that the Quiet would leave, but it didn't. It was a little up and down the first few days but became calm and steady, and she began to feel safe. She didn't know why, she couldn't explain it, so she didn't try. It was so much better than what she had had, so she just accepted it, it was a gift after all. After a few more days she started to relax, she began to feel grateful the storm had somehow passed and after maybe a week or two she was able to let go just a little and breathe again.

As soon as she was able she got back to work. She knew sitting around wasn't the answer, her sanity was at stake, and she wasn't sure she could take another tornado ripping through her mind. She was soon asked to work on a commercial for Motorola. It was the early 1990s, and cell phones were still an uncommon luxury, not to mention they were the size of a brick! It was a print campaign to go in magazines and on billboards, and she jumped at the chance. The idea was that if you had a cell phone you were as free as a bird, little did we all know back then how free we were without them! Deborah and the rest of the small crew were hired to make various human-sized bird wings that could be blended into the clothes of the models to make them look as if they could take flight. A young woman in a swimsuit would be sitting on an exotic beach with parrot wings emerging from her back and a businessman whose trench coat was flapping open blended into eagle wings, each holding their cell phones as they took flight to freedom. It was a fun 3-week project, and everyone knew that it was going to be shot on the tropical island of Martinique, but who would go? The two bosses were of course going, and they decided that the four-person crew would pick straws for the other two places. Deborah wasn't too attached to the outcome. Sure it would be amazing to go, but she knew it was only fair that Sue who had more experience should, and besides, she wasn't comfortable yet about being so far from home. She was still nervous about getting around and very conscious of the Quiet and what a precious gift it was, so when she pulled the wrong straw it was ok with her to stay home.

Sue was wonderful, she had worked on the movies *Labyrinth* and *Dark Crystal* and was really generous with her experience and skills, with none of that competitiveness or weirdness that Deborah had experienced with many others in this creative freelance world. They had hit it off straight away, Sue was older with two daughters about Deborah's own age, and so she felt safe with her. As they got to work on the wings surrounded by feathers, glue, thread, and wire, the two women talked and shared stories about their lives. Finally, she felt safe enough to confide in Sue about the recent mugging.

"Have you ever talked to someone about it, you know, a professional?" she inquired with concern.

"I was sent to a psychiatrist in Manchester after the second one, but she didn't have a clue, the stupid cow just kept on asking me about the attack! My problem was that I couldn't stop thinking about the attack and needed help to learn how to not to! She was useless, so I gave up and struggled on my own."

"Ok," offered Sue, compassionately stroking her arm, "so I have another idea. I have a friend who runs the Women in Crisis Center in North London; would you like to talk to her? She is amazing and knows all about this kind of stuff. I'll get you her number."

Shelly was a character. Born in Hungary, she had fled to England as a young child with her family after the war. She had seen and experienced more crisis in her lifetime than anyone should, and yet spent her time helping women who needed understanding and support. Shelly invited Deborah to her home for a chat, and so began a friendship that would last for over thirty years.

Deborah was very nervous, a little unsure of what she was letting herself in for as she knocked on Shelly's door. She had argued with herself all day about cancelling, and so there had been a lot of *Shut up* shouting in her head even as the front door opened.

"Deborah? Please come in." There was something comforting in Shelley's faint Eastern European accent. "Sue told me a little bit about you, and I'm so interested to hear more." She showed Deborah to an armchair in the living room. It was a modest two-bedroom flat, with a hint of pre-war Hungarian decor, but she was immediately struck by the young man asleep on the sofa. He was wearing a black suit, white shirt, a yarmulke, and white strings were hanging from his waist.

"Hey! Rabbi, wake up, time to go!" shouted Shelly as the young man rose sluggishly to his feet. "Hymie is waiting for you in the car!" Deborah felt she had entered another world. "My husband, Hymie, works the night shift at the Chabad men's recovery house, so we won't be disturbed. You would like some tea?"

"Thanks. Does the Rabbi work there too?" asked Deborah innocently.

"Him? No, he's a heroin addict just flew in from Belgium to get clean. Milk, sugar?"

"Oh! Uh, yes, thank you. When do you get to see each other?" asked Deborah feeling a bit out of place.

Shelly laughed as she came back from the kitchen with two mugs of tea and a big smile.

"Some of the best marriages work this way. Now, tell me all about you."

Deborah sat back in the comfy armchair and told Shelly what had happened. She had told it over so many times in her head and quite a few times to other people since she had been in London, usually to get sympathy or attention, so by now she knew exactly how to pace it and where to put the emphasis for maximum effect. But Shelly's reaction was not what she was expecting.

"Are you ready to let go of your story?"

"What?" blurted out Deborah in astonishment. She had expected tea and sympathy. Here was the tea, but where was the sympathy? She could tell Shelly wasn't trying to be unkind, she had listened very intently, but Deborah was taken aback by her question. "I don't understand, are you saying I made all that up?"

"No, not all," said Shelly gently, "but I think you are very attached to it? Don't worry I totally understand, I used to be very attached to my story too. I am the child of Holocaust Survivors, my parents couldn't parent me, they could hardly look after themselves. I had a tough childhood looking after myself and my brother, the type that would make you cry if I told you all the details, but with the help of some very kind people I began to see that it was killing me to hold on to it and it had served its purpose."

"I don't understand," said Deborah.

"That's ok," continued Shelly. "I didn't either at first, it took me a while. I was very stubborn, but you are smart and you will see."

"See what?" Deborah felt even more confused. She felt threatened and was starting to regret coming.

"You will see that these violent attacks happened

to you, but they are not you. They don't define who you are unless you let them. They have become a story that you tell to comfort yourself." Deborah was stunned. She sat in silence trying to take this in. Was Shelly more stupid than the psychiatrist?!

"But it did happen, exactly as I said, and it's no comfort!"

"I know," agreed Shelly smiling at her, "and it hurt you very deeply. But something even deeper inside you wants to live, and that very wise part of you is ready to let go of the past and move on."

"How do you know, you just met me?"

"Because you showed up here tonight."

Deborah stared at the floor for a few minutes. She knew Shelly was being kind, it just wasn't what she was expecting. They talked a little more, but Shelly wouldn't be drawn into it any further, and so they agreed to meet again. "Come down to the Center next week, I want to show you what we do there." Deborah agreed as Shelly walked with her to the door.

"What's that?" asked Deborah as she pointed to a small, rectangular box on the frame of the door.

Shelly laughed, "It's a Mezuzah! What kind of Jew are you?"

Deborah shrugged. "I don't know, my parents never talked about it. Actually, they didn't talk very much at all."

"How did it go?" inquired Sue eagerly the next day in the workshop.

"I'm not sure, she was...interesting."

"Yep, that's one way to put it," agreed Sue with a smile as she lit up a cigarette. "So I have some good news!"

"Yeah? What's happening?"

"I just got taken on to another movie!"

"That's great!" exclaimed Deborah.

"Wanna join me?"

"What??" stuttered Deborah excitedly.

"I'm gonna need an assistant, so I want you to meet the project supervisor," said Sue nonchalantly, as if working on Hollywood movies was something that happens every day. "It's gonna shoot in L.A., Spielberg is producing, and we will be working for Jim Henson's Creature Shop making all the um," she took a drag on her cigarette, "you know, all the creatures."

"Spielberg as in...Steven? Jim Henson as in Kermit and Miss Piggy, and L.A. as in...Hollywood?" gasped Deborah in total disbelief.

"Yes, but don't pack your bags just yet. I think we will just be the building crew here in London. They have a workshop and crew out in L.A."

"Uh, sure, ok!"

Deborah couldn't believe it, she was blown away, jobs like this were just dreams. It was almost unbelievable...!

4
Islington

1991

Deborah walked out of the Holloway Road Underground, the nearest station to the Islington Crisis Center. She didn't feel in any kind of crisis right at that moment but was intrigued to talk to Shelly some more. The Quiet had stayed, and it was becoming more normal to have it around. It was like having a calm new roommate who had replaced the old noisy one with much better habits and friends. It was about 8:30 p.m. and the streets were still wet from a rain shower that had drenched the evening rush hour. The address took her to a doorway between two shops on Islington High Street. One was a newsagent that was still open, selling newspapers, cigarettes, the usual birthday cards, and sweets, and on the other side was an Oxfam charity shop that had already closed for the night. She walked nervously up the narrow wooden stairs as two women came down, pushing past her. She wondered if it wasn't too late to turn around, maybe they had the right idea? At the top of the stairs, there was a room with an old sofa, and a coffee table smothered with leaflets and handouts. On the walls were various posters about hotlines and support services, self help groups, and events, and one very sad looking spider plant sitting on a small, dusty shelf. It was just like Deborah had imagined, rundown, and cozy.

Shelly was in her office surrounded by piles of paper, filing cabinets, and overflowing ashtrays. She got up and came forward to hug Deborah, and immediately Deborah started to cry.

"I don't know why I'm crying," sobbed Deborah, embarrassingly wiping away the tears. "I'm actually having a great day, I just got some great news, I'm so sorry… I don't know why I'm crying, I never do this."

"You let it out, my dear. Cry all you want," Shelley handed Deborah a box of tissues. "You have been holding it together for a very long time, and the good news probably let you breathe for a moment I think, no?"

"Maybe…" Deborah swallowed hard and tried to regain her composure. She wasn't used to showing any weakness or being the vulnerable one. They sat for a few moments, Deborah staring at the threadbare carpet, regretting that she had come. Shelly spoke first.

"A misunderstanding most of us have is that we feel uncomfortable because of people or situations. *My husband makes me so angry*, or *This office is so disorganized, it drives me crazy!*" Shelly fell back in her chair laughing at her own examples. "It always seems that it's because of what's happening out there that determines how we feel."

"It isn't?" Deborah sheepishly wiped her face.

"No, let's think about it. If I believe that you or they or it are responsible for how I feel, then I'm in for a lifetime of hard work spinning plates and controlling people so that I can feel okay. It's impossible to get everyone and everything to behave, and so with that belief, I'm never going to be ok!"

"I'm exhausted," sighed Deborah.

"I'm not surprised. Trying to be perfect, the hero, the better person, is a lot of hard work."

Deborah thought about it for a moment. "If you

mean I need to think positive, I've been trying that."

Shelly smiled and shook her head. "Thinking positive is a great idea, but it rarely has any permanent effect. It's a bit like pouring pink paint on rotten wood; it will look pretty for a while, but the rot is still there underneath."

Deborah looked up. She looked down. She was stumped, a thousand thoughts were trying to push their way through her head. "But...aren't we supposed to think positive, be positive? So, then what am I supposed to do with all this?" She pointed at her head in exasperation.

Shelly smiled, "We all have old ideas, ideas that sometimes seem like a good idea at the time but if you look underneath they are usually driven by fear. I'm suggesting that it's an old idea that other people or situations have to change for us to be ok."

"What fear is underneath thinking positive?" Deborah felt completely baffled.

Shelly gave a dramatic shrug of her shoulders, "Probably something like, *if I let go then the darkness will engulf me*?"

"It did, after my last attack my thinking was raging, I couldn't get a break, and it beat me up every day! I was so scared that if I let go, I would go down and not be able to get back up!"

Shelly smiled and nodded in agreement.

"It was so bad that I used to tell myself to...shut up," Deborah spoke cautiously. She had never told anyone about how she yelled at herself and was nervous about Shelly's reaction.

"That's good," reassured Shelly.

"Good?" Deborah was a little surprised.

"Yes, that was something deep inside you fighting to survive."

"Really? I was always afraid to tell anyone as I wasn't sure it was, well, very healthy? I mean yelling at yourself is kind of nuts, they lock you up for stuff like that, I just didn't know what else to do."

Shelly smiled and reached into a drawer for a piece of paper. "Can I ask you to take a look at this? We are starting a new training program next week for counsellors, and I want you to consider it?"

"But I thought you asked me here to...to offer me some help?"

"I am, Deborah; and I think the best help I can give you is to offer you the chance to start thinking about other people. You have been thinking about yourself for a very long time now, and that thinking is just going round and round, it's hurting you, it's time for something different."

Deborah wasn't sure. She immediately had huge doubts that she could help anybody, she was barely out of the woods herself! But Shelly clearly thought it was a good idea and could see something in her that she hoped Deborah would soon see for herself, that letting go was the best thing that could have happened to her and now she could start again.

It was about 10 p.m. when she walked back along Holloway Road toward the underground station. The newsagent had shut, and the streets were quiet. Deborah felt different. She wasn't sure what or why, she just knew something was different.

5
Camden

1992

The meeting with the project supervisor at Jim Henson's Creature Shop went very well. The workshop was located in a dilapidated old Victorian Warehouse that overlooked the canals at trendy Camden Lock. It was a maze of workshops and studios, one room after another of fascinating people building fantastical creatures and puppets that could talk, snarl, and smile. Mold makers covered in plaster, fabricators surrounded by foam and latex, and computer geeks with who knows what latest gadget on workbenches overflowing with wire and cables. Norman offered her the job on the spot and signed her up as Sue's assistant to make the animatronics on the new movie production of *The Flintstones*. She was excited, it was so exciting, it was her first movie and it was a pure gift. Henson's was making all the dinosaurs and creatures for the film, and Sue and Deborah were signed up to make all the birds: the Dictabird, the Record Playing Bird, and various others. A few days after she had started, they were all called into the conference room for a design meeting. Around the table were an unusual collection of artists, computer geeks, mechanics, and designers. She felt wholly inadequate, like an imposter, as she listened to them discussing the intricacies of the project. Many of her new colleagues had been doing this amazing kind of movie work for

years. She later found out that several of them were
Oscar winners! She was just waiting for someone to
realise that she shouldn't be there and ask her to leave
when she noticed, on the wall behind Norman, a very
large black-and-white iconic photographic print of the
late Jim Henson with Kermit the Frog looking
encouragingly over his shoulder. Deborah felt a surge
of gratitude run through her whole body, she had been
so close to not making it and now here she was sitting
with some of the most talented people in the country,
maybe the world. *How did that happen*, she kept
wondering…

Over the next three months, Sue taught her all the
techniques she needed to be part of the team, and
together they made the most wonderful fantastical
creatures. By day she worked in the world of fantasy
and illusion, and twice a week at night she dived into
the counsellor training that would turn her own dark
experience into miraculous light. Shelly was in charge
of running the office and hotline, and her colleague,
Francesca, was in charge of training and fundraising.
Francesca was a Londoner, tough and streetwise. She
had survived a violent marriage and had made it her
life's mission to help and educate women so that they
didn't have to suffer as she had. She had spent the 80s
in New York where she had hung out with the
infamous feminist Gloria Steinem and many other
courageous women fighting for women's rights.

The other five women on the course were all ages
and backgrounds, and they were all being trained to
answer the hotline, counsel one-on-one, and do
presentations for social workers, nurses, and
community groups. The classes with Francesca were
always interesting and thought-provoking, and it
became routine for Deborah to need a chat with Shelly
after each one; something always came up that needed
to be explored further.

"Shelly, what did Francesca mean when she said *the only thing suffering cannot stand is being seen with clarity*? I mean it sounds like she is saying suffering is something of an illusion?" Something had resonated with Deborah and she wanted to know more.

"That's exactly what she is saying, but I would never advocate that you tell a brand new client that; that would be heartless! But it's still true nonetheless. Because suffering is an illusion created by the mind, like we were talking about before, most of us want to focus on what the other person did wrong or the government or whatever, but it's an illusion that anyone can make us feel anything; it's always our reaction to life that determines how we feel."

"When I first met you, you said something about me letting go of my story. Is Francesca saying the same thing?"

"Yes. I heard once that suffering is to the mind like pain is to the body." Shelley sat back in her chair. "When we have pain in our bodies it's the bodies way of letting us know that we should take our hand out of the fire, or drink some water because we are dehydrated, for example. It's the amazing way humans are designed. Mental or emotional suffering is the same thing for your mind; it's a message that you are looking outside yourself for the answers."

Deborah still couldn't comprehend that it wasn't real. The memories of all those days and nights reliving the attack, crying herself to sleep, and waking up with no reason to go on living, she could still feel the pain.

"If you're anything like me, you are now thinking that we are all crazy and telling you either it didn't hurt or it didn't happen or get over it?"

"Yes," confessed Deborah sheepishly, "but *it* did happen, *it* did hurt and I *can't* get over it!"

"I know, these ideas are very threatening to the ego," offered Shelly, "which is why it's not the first thing you want to say to a new client." She continued cautiously, "You listen carefully and patiently and help them see this is true for themselves. Many people are invested in their suffering and it's very disconcerting at first to be asked to let go of it. It's like being asked to let go of their child. Some of us have nurtured and protected our suffering for a long time, we have become so identified with it that it feels like it is us. I remember thinking, *Who will I be if I let go of this? Will you like me if I don't have some terrible story to impress you with or to get you to feel sorry for me?* Your job, Deborah, is to help them see that they are not their trauma, or that the crisis doesn't define them. We want to help them have real insights that will give them long-lasting recovery, not those calorie-empty, feel-good bumper-stickers that will make them hungry again in an hour or two. People usually come to us full of blame and anger, but we want to help them see that they can be ok despite what happened to them, or even in the situation they have now. We want them to see that when their mind quiets down, they can heal, get free of it and find out who they really are."

"Is that what you are trying to do with me?"

Shelly smiled. "Your acute suffering was a while ago in Manchester and had you come to me then I would have hugged you and loved you and told you to cry as much as you needed until you felt safe enough to go deeper. But you pulled yourself out of that pit on your own, your inner strength helped you survive and so I think helping others do the same will help you understand yourself even better now." There was a pause and then Shelly explained with deep kindness, "You may find what you are experiencing now, this sadness, is a grieving for that young woman who had to go through such an experience."

Deborah felt emotions filling up her eyes. She knew it was true even if she didn't quite understand it yet. The resistance was still there, but she wanted to push forward.

"What do I do now?"

Shelley turned to the bookshelf behind her and searched until she located a tiny, little book. "Have you ever read this?" She handed Deborah a copy of Viktor Frankl's *Man's Search for Meaning*.

"Nope."

She flipped through the pages "I can't find it right now but somewhere in here I think there's that famous quote *Between stimulus and response, there is a space. In that space is our power to choose our response. In our response lies our growth and our freedom.* Do you see what Frankl is saying? He is telling us that we don't have to accept our first reaction, our first thoughts are not always the truth about the way things really are, we can choose to have a good life if we want! Borrow it, I think it might help. He writes with such understanding and kindness, you know."

Back at work things were going great. Sue was sharing all her skills and know-how and it was exciting to be learning so many new techniques. Everything they were making was a prototype, everything had to be invented and designed down to the last detail, tried and retried until it worked really well. Weeks and weeks of work were going into the most magical creations. First sculptors led by Larry created the basic shape of the animal so that a mould could be made in fiberglass for them all to work from. Next, the mechanics would make a very detailed moving skeleton with intricate mechanisms to support a fabricated body. Computer geniuses like Mitch were working hard to perfect the technology that would enable the creatures to move by remote control according to the puppeteer's wishes, and then Sue, Deborah, and their team would give them the finishing details of fur and feathers, latex skins, and glassy eyes and eyelashes. It was thrilling to be working with the best mechanics and fabricators, computer geniuses, and artists of all kinds. It was a true collaboration and as the weeks turned into months, they perfected fabulous animatronic puppets that were going to be shipped to Los Angeles for filming.

"Do you ever get attached to the creatures you make?"

"Kind of," laughed Sue as they worked away attaching feathers to the wing mechanism of a prehistoric looking bird. "I mean, if one of them got trashed, I wouldn't cry like it was one of my kids but it would be a damn waste of all that hard work."

The birds that they were making could flap their wings, talk, and turn their eyes to look straight at you and with the cunning tricks of lighting and camera work and the talents of an expert puppeteer, these creatures would come to life and fool the most cynical of viewers.

"I always think that making fantasy creatures is easy, though," said Sue.

"Easy?" repeated Deborah, astonished. "This is some of the most exacting work I have ever done!"

"Wait till you get asked to make a copy of a real animal, then you will know what exacting is. Making fantasy creatures is relatively easy by comparison. No one can tell you an alien is the wrong shade of green or too big or too small, it's all up to the imagination. But making a copy of a cat or a gorilla, well, it has to be perfect because everyone knows what a cat or gorilla looks like and they will happily tell you if it's wrong. To make something that everyone knows is not possible like a dog talking or a gorilla playing poker now that's a real challenge."

Deborah couldn't imagine it, she was having so much fun it didn't matter what was coming next.

6
Islington 2

1992

"**O**ccasionally you will get a client who is not exactly who they say they are," cautioned Francesca at the next class. "Be aware. Sometimes clients will try to manipulate you, and you will have to be on your guard against being used,"

"Why would someone do that?" asked Susie innocently.

"For many reasons," explained Francesca. "Sometimes it's for attention, sometimes to get revenge, and sometimes it's for money."

"Money?" questioned Nicola.

"Yes, money. There is 'disability,' and a thing called the Criminal Injuries Compensation Board. If they receive proof of injury or trauma, then there is money to be dished out. We can put clients in touch with them if necessary and help them with the paperwork, but there is a temptation to exaggerate, even falsify. Money is a very seductive thing, and vulnerable people can be manipulated or be manipulating to get it. The difficulty with post-traumatic cases is that they are what we call 'self-reporting,' and there are no objective signs. Think about it, if someone cries and is hysterical, does that mean they have suffered more than others? More than someone who is quiet and withdrawn?"

"I got some money after I was attacked in

Manchester," said Deborah.

"Oh, you poor poor thing," oozed Suzie sending Deborah a big air hug. Deborah ignored her and continued, "but I don't remember filling out any paperwork...?"

"Did you give any kind of statement?" asked Francesca.

"Yes, but just to some spotty young idiot of a police detective."

"Then he must have sent it in for you."

Deborah froze. She hated that man with such an intensity that her brain couldn't compute Francesca's words. She hated him for his insensitivity, the way he had dismissed her, even the way he looked, his hair, his voice. She had spent years going over and over how he treated her as if she was expendable, that she was just an inconvenience in his world. The combination of the people who had walked by and not stopped and the policeman dismissing her had tormented and tortured her soul. She couldn't imagine he could possibly be the one who had helped her. As soon as class was over she went straight to Shelly's flat trying not to panic, her thoughts were flying everywhere like crazy jumping jack firecrackers.

"I can't believe it!" cried Deborah, "I have hated that man every day for six years! I have relived and relived that conversation. He had the nerve to tell me that going after the guys that attacked me wasn't high on his list of priorities! He basically told me that I didn't count for anything!"

"I know," sympathised Shelley, "but do you see how this story has held you prisoner to a memory, and the truth was that he did something to try to help you and without needing your thanks?"

"Is that what you meant when I first met you, about letting go of my story?"

"Yes, partly," admitted Shelly. "You needed

someone to blame, you needed to understand something that didn't make any sense to you at the time."

Deborah caught her breath and fell silent for a few minutes. She could feel the heaviness of the story lifting and felt the Quiet taking its place. Then she remembered something from the book Shelly had given her.

"You mean like Viktor Frankl said in his book?" Deborah responded, now sitting up, "*It is the mental agony caused by the injustice, the unreasonableness of it all.*"[1]

"Ooooh, listen to you quoting Viktor Frankl," quipped Shelly with a smile.

"But it made so much sense to me, it jumped off the page when I read it!" exclaimed Deborah. "The injustice of it all was more than I could bear. I just couldn't get my head around that, why they picked on me, why the passers-by didn't stop to help, why they just kept on walking while I was screaming for my life, and that policeman who said I wasn't important enough to bother with. If I could have just understood it, I think I wouldn't have become so sick and crazy."

"Frankl quotes Nietzsche in that book I think, something like, '*If a man can understand the why, then he can bear almost any how,*'[2] or something like that. Anyway, what he means is that understanding makes intolerable things easier and although it may be true, that just wasn't available to you at the time, and your mind took it very hard. Now that you know that *idiot* policeman actually took time to fill in paperwork that got you, how much compensation?"

"Six hundred quid."

"Six hundred pounds?! Wow! So how do you feel about him now?"

"A little better," answered Deborah, with a vague hint of a smile.

Shelly smiled. "Think about this for a moment. What if you could change your view of someone or something without new information like this, now that would be priceless wouldn't it?"

"What do you mean?"

"Well this information has shifted your view of him, and you feel a little better. You are having a new experience of what happened. What if you could do that for yourself? What if you could let go of the negative stuff by just being open to other possibilities, by being willing to let go of old ideas?"

"You mean choose new thoughts?" wondered Deborah.

"Kind of," offered Shelly. "Frankl chose to think about his wife and focused on publishing his work, and that carried him through the nightmare of the Nazi murder camps. He was in the most hellish of experiences, and he chose to direct his attention to the positive so that he had something to live for. There's a lot of research about this. Did you know that in every army and major police force there is a team of people who have the God-forsaken job of picking up body parts after an accident or a suicide? You would think that these brave men and women would all be suffering from what they have just decided to call PTSD."

"What's that?" asked Deborah.

"It's a new diagnosis they just came up with, Post-Traumatic Stress Disorder. Francesca will give you a class on it I'm sure. Now, I'm not saying that these people picking up body parts are all super well and happy, but they don't, in general, suffer too much because they are doing such a noble job; the heroic mission they are on gives them the inner resources, the resilience to cope."

"Wow," exclaimed Deborah, "that's amazing!"

"Yes, but as we said before, replacing negative

thinking with positive thinking only takes you so far, like the pink-paint treatment. It looks good for a while, but eventually, the rot will come through again. You were pouring pink paint on your very painful thoughts about what happened, but what if you had understood that blaming is not the answer and looked inside instead?" explained Shelly.

"What do you mean?"

"Well, in my experience, I started to understand that it was actually the story that I was telling myself, over and over, that was bringing me down. The war, what the Nazis did to my family, or whatever event that I thought was causing my distress wasn't happening anymore; it was over and I was now safe. Once I saw that to be true, I naturally moved into a better place. Once I saw for myself that no one had to change for me to be ok, that it was my old ideas and reactions to them that was hurting me, then I started to get better," grinned Shelly. "If I'm the one thinking the old ideas, then I can choose better ones." The two women sat quietly for a moment. "Have you ever seen The Wizard of Oz?"

"Yes, a long time ago." Deborah wondered where the conversation was going now.

"I think the Wizard of Oz is a very spiritual movie," ventured Shelly. "You know how Dorothy is running all over Oz looking for a way to get back home? She asks the Tin Man, the Lion, and the Scarecrow how she can get back to Kansas, right?" Deborah nodded. "At the end of the movie, Glinda the Good Witch says, "Click your heels together, Dorothy, and you can go home.""

"I get it," acknowledged Deborah, "she had the answer with her all the time!"

"Yes, but that's not all. If you keep watching, Dorothy says, "but why didn't you tell me before?" and Glinda says, "because you wouldn't have believed me.""

Deborah looked at Shelly. She sat with a quiet mind for a moment and then smiled. "You are right, I couldn't have heard this before. The psychiatrist, the policeman, my friends couldn't help me because my thinking was so focused on the injustice of what happened to me."

"Yes. You weren't ready, but it was there with you all the time. Now can I ask you a question?"

"Sure!" Deborah was a little surprised.

"Are you ready to forgive him, the policeman I mean?"

Deborah was a bit taken aback, she had almost forgotten that it was because of him that she had run to Shelly's flat that night. She thought about him for a moment. She remembered his face, his sallow almost grey skin and pale, reddish hair. Her mind softened as she sighed heavily.

"Yes."

The classes with Francesca continued. They learned about legal matters, different resources, and benefits that clients could apply for; they even took a CPR course, but her favorite classes were always the ones about how to help clients get free of their suffering.

"Let's get started. Julie just called to say she is running late and will be here soon," declared Francesca.

"That woman needs to get her ducks in a row, she is always late," whispered Nicola.

"Honey, her ducks aren't even in the same pond!" sniggered Susie, and Francesca tried not to laugh as she continued.

"Now, I know I keep suggesting books, but this is a long-time favourite of mine. It was published in the late 70s but *The Road Less Traveled* is still very relevant for us in 1992," informed Francesca. "Peck says, '*You cannot truly listen to anyone and do anything else at the same time.* '3 Now, that seems pretty obvious, but how many of us are thinking about what to cook for dinner or, I hope I don't miss the last bus or, Crikey, this person is so boring, when are they going to get to the point?!" Everyone laughed, they all knew they had done it. "But your listening skills are going to make the difference between an ok counsellor and a great one."

"Ok so what if the person is rambling on and on, isn't that enabling? Shouldn't we be offering solutions?" challenged Nicola.

"Your heart is in the right place, but could you see that if you are just waiting for them to shut up so you can tell them what they need to do, then you weren't really listening?"

"No. You just quoted that guy who said we shouldn't be doing anything else like, I dunno, writing a shopping list or looking at the bus timetable. That would be rude, I get that. I'm listening for their problems so I can offer solutions," insisted Nicola almost commanding approval.

"But how can you hear, really hear what their problem is if you are already coming up with solutions?" urged Francesca.

Nicola bristled. "I don't get it, I thought we were here to offer help. You know, affirmations, validation, solutions?" She sat back in her chair with her arms folded and looked at the rest of the group for some validation for herself.

"Yes, we want to help, but sometimes we can jump to conclusions of what we think they need when we haven't really listened to what they really need. Needing to be the one in control is one of the things that can stop us from really listening. For example, if they witnessed a fatal accident or uh, their teenage daughter is pregnant, don't start talking about that time you saw an accident or your friend got pregnant in high school. It's not about you, it's never about you. We want to connect with our clients. Sympathy and solutions might seem like the logical thing, but it actually pushes a kind of wedge between you and the client. It's so easy to make a judgement — only we call it 'offering solutions' — when most of the time, in my experience, what people really want is to know they are going to be ok. That's real connection."

"So how do you do that?" asked Susie, "I mean, what if it's not going to be ok? Sometimes it just isn't!"

"Notice I said, they *are* going to be ok, not *it?* We have no idea what or how the situation is going to unfold but helping your client to see that they are ok, that they have all the resilience and inner strength they need to cope, that's worth millions."

"I still don't get it," challenged Nicola. "I mean if someone's sitting in front of you and they are sobbing their heart out about having just lost their husband, or they were mugged or whatever, how can you say they are going to be ok? We don't know that!"

"You are right, we don't know how the circumstances are going to turn out, but if you listen carefully enough and wait, I bet you will hear them come to some conclusion themselves about what is best for them. They know you care because you are really listening and fully present. And when you are really listening, not paying attention to your own ideas, you will be inspired to help in a way that is right for them."

Everyone sat for a moment.

"You mean if I'm not thinking about what I think they should do or what I should say, something will just magically come to me? Like an angel is going to whisper in my ear the right thing to say? Wow that's super cool!" declared Andrea excitedly.

"Yes! Exactly!! I'm not suggesting you just sit there like a lump and do the nodding dog thing and then show them the door. Just be aware of the quality of your listening. Are you judging? Are you waiting for them to shut up so you can put them straight? Are you daydreaming? It can happen to the best of us. But once you catch yourself, come back and listen a bit more with nothing on your mind. You will be surprised by what new, inspired ideas that angel can put into your mind. That's how real transformation happens, not from the words you are using but from the place where the words come from."

7
Shoreditch

Two days after she had finished the training at the Islington Women in Crisis Center, Deborah got a call from Shelly, saying she had a client for her and could she come in to meet her? Deborah was instantly nervous and full of doubt. What if she didn't have the right answers? What if she said the wrong thing? What if she messed up? A heavy feeling fell over her, and she started to think of ways she could get out of it. Suddenly, she became acutely aware of her thoughts. Her thinking had immediately gone off into outer space without her permission like it always did, which was always followed by that sinking feeling. She was used to the sinking feeling, but she had never heard her thoughts before, not really heard them like they were speaking on a radio separate from her. Before that, she had always believed that her thoughts were her and so they needed to be listened to, discussed, analyzed, and told to shut up when they misbehaved, but she wondered for a minute how much thinking actually goes on without her noticing. Wow, this is new.

"Just share what you know," advised Shelly on the phone. "You paint, right? Well if I was learning to paint, would you suggest I work endlessly on one painting till it was perfect or went out and painted lots of different pictures, making mistakes and seeing what works best?" Shelly didn't wait for an answer. "The painter who tries lots of things will be the better painter right? Don't think you have to wait to get it right, we all make mistakes, it's part of learning. Do your best, and you will learn like we all did."

Deborah still wasn't sure, making mistakes was one of her biggest fears and going into the unknown was her biggest fear of all. New places, new people, and now she was dealing with other people's lives! She could feel her herself getting anxious, but, curiously, she wasn't bothered by it. Deborah's mind cleared and instead, she focused on Shelly's calm confidence just like Francesca had taught them would happen.

Shelly continued, "Look, you have been through some very traumatic experiences and have understood how to be free of them. People can pick up on that and will sense that you have something real to offer. If you really believe that she can get better and share that from your heart, she will trust you... I trust you."

"Thank you." Deborah started to relax as a beautiful feeling of calm came over her.

"And remember, listen really well. All most of us really need is someone to listen. You'll be fine."

It was a Wednesday night, Deborah grabbed something from a sandwich shop after work and made her way to the Center. She was still a bit nervous, or was it excitement?

"She will be here in a few minutes. Now, she is a bit of a mess, but she will tell you all about it. Her name is Stephanie," said Shelly, with a big, encouraging smile.

Stephanie and Deborah went into one of the counseling rooms and sat on the big, squishy sofa together. She was about the same age as Deborah, a natural, soft blonde with pale, clear skin and soft blue eyes. She looked as innocent as could be and in a very refined English way, she launched straight into her story without any prompting.

"I'm detoxing myself from a very high dose of Prozac. I've done this a few times now so don't freak out if I get a bit you know, lost. I just need someone to hold on to right now." She patted Deborah's arm reassuringly, which was strange as Deborah thought she was there to reassure her. "So forgive me for my bluntness, but I've had to tell this horrible story over so many times, and I'm, well, whatever, here goes." Deborah was partly in awe and somewhat relieved that so far she hadn't had to say anything.

"My parents were diplomats, and they were often posted to distant and exotic places when I was young. On one of those postings, we stayed in a large house on the edge of a city and the housekeeper took it upon herself to sell me to the local freaks and criminally insane, who would pick me up in a big, black limo and take me out to the jungle where they made me the star of their sick ritual sex ceremonies. I was sexually abused from the age of three to five and of course, they told me that if I told anyone, they would kill my parents and clearly, they knew where I lived. So, I stuffed it all deep inside, I guess hoping it would come to an end one day. Finally, we moved, and it was over. Then when I was about 16, I started dating boys, and of course, all the memories came flooding out, and I freaked out big time. I was having nightmares, I couldn't eat or sleep. My poor parents were freaking out trying to work out what to do with me. They took me to every psychiatrist and therapist who knew or thought they knew anything about child sexual abuse from here to New York and back again. They put me in a looney bin on and off, and in fact, they want me to go back in one now. I have two researchers working on my case, and the shrinks keep pumping me full of meds. I tell them I don't want any of it, but my parents feel so guilty that they don't want me to feel any more pain or hurt myself. Problem is, I don't feel anything when I'm on all that stuff, and my life is going by. I've lost so much of it already. I just want them to leave me alone." She sat back on the sofa exhausted by her story and stared up at the ceiling in frustration and despair.

Deborah was on the edge of her seat, literally. She had no experience with any of this, the abuse, the meds, the treatments. She tried to remember everything she had learned, especially to listen. She wanted to ask her if she was ready to let go of the story like Shelly had said to her, but didn't have the nerve. Instead, she expressed her sympathy and asked what did Stephanie need right now.

"Wow, nobody ever asks me that," responded Stephanie, still staring at the ceiling. "Most people, shrinks that is, ask me to tell them more gruesome details about what happened and ask me how I feel about it. How do they think I feel? I'm angry, I'm hurt, and I'm sick of it!"

"Do you have anyone besides your parents and shrinks to talk to about all this?"

"Not really, I have a younger sister. She wasn't touched, thank God, she was just a baby, but she is traumatised by this too, as my parents haven't had much time for her while they freak out over me. We have moved around so much that I never really made friends. Can you imagine it? 'Hi, I'm Stephanie, I was sexually abused in a jungle freak show, and now I'm a broken mess, wanna hang out tonight?' The only people who want to hang out with me are equally screwy or want to play the hero and save me, so no, I don't." She sighed again and closed her eyes.

"So you have us now, we are on your side, whatever it is you need," reassured Deborah, her heart filling up with tears as she tried to fumble for words.

"Thanks," said Stephanie quietly.

The two young women sat for a while, and then Deborah said, "I would imagine that digging around in the past all the time is excruciating?"

"Yes, very. I don't know why they always insist on that. I think some of them are so fascinated that it's kind of like entertainment for them. I'm always the freak show for everyone to gawp at." Stephanie made a noise like someone vomiting.

"Can I ask? Are you still having flashbacks?" asked Deborah, gently.

"Sometimes. That's why they give me the meds, although my thinking is always all over the place so detoxing from them doesn't help. I can be on the bus, and suddenly I don't know where I am, and then I have a panic attack, and then they want to fill me up with more meds and send me off to the looney bin again. I feel like I'm on a damn hamster wheel."

"You are safe here, and if you ever get panicked or lost, you can call me."

"Thank you."

Deborah and Stephanie worked out that they should meet twice a week for a few weeks and see how the whole detox thing went. She called once from a public phone box in Kensington in a panic, but Deborah was able to reassure her, and somehow she found the courage to get herself home. The next few times they met, Stephanie was very scattered and just needed a place to come and be safe. After about two weeks, she seemed to be more stable, and they were able to talk.

"I've been thinking about what you said about my thinking attacking me. Sometimes it just comes, and I can't stop it," apologised Stephanie.

"I know it seems that way. When I was recovering from my attack, I kept finding myself in the middle of this big retelling of the story all the time, and it was as if my thoughts were coming in at me from all directions. I walked around with this imaginary audience in my head that I needed to tell it to, over and over again."

"Exactly! Sometimes it feels like my head is stuck in a snow globe!" cried Stephanie, and the two women laughed hysterically. It was so good to laugh.

Deborah took a deep breath, "Can I ask you something?"

"Sure."

"Are you ready to let go of the story?" Deborah was nervous that she would scare her off but hoped that they had built up enough trust to try.

"What do you mean?"

"Shelly asked me this when I first met her, and I was confused, too. It felt like she was telling me it didn't hurt or that I should get over it, but she helped me to see that I didn't need it anymore."

Stephanie hesitated. "You know, sometimes I think I could lecture in child abuse treatment. I have been treated for longer than some of these professionals have studied it. It's almost like I have become a professional patient." She was very calm as she said this, almost with relief to get it out. Deborah smiled at her honesty.

"Looking back, I saw that my attack had become part of my identity," shared Deborah, hoping it would help Stephanie to open up to the idea that she could let go. "Clearly you didn't have any part in what happened to you as a child. I didn't have any part in what happened to me when those three men jumped me from behind. But as I got more honest with myself, I saw that I had a part in what I was doing with it now. I was using it for self-pity, for attention..." Deborah paused to see if Stephanie was still with her. Cautiously she added, "and I used it to manipulate people."

"Oooo, yes," agreed Stephanie emphatically. She paused again and then blurted out, "It's almost like...like I have become..." She stopped as her eyes started to dart about, Deborah hoped it was in excitement, maybe a breakthrough and not a psychotic episode.

"Oh my gosh, oh my gosh!" said Stephanie in her delightful way. "I am...I am the Queen of Child Abuse!"

Deborah fell back in amazement as Stephanie almost vibrated with her realization.

"I am the Queen of Child Abuse!" repeated Stephanie. "No one can top my story, no one is allowed to be mean to me, I can get anyone, everyone to listen to me and do exactly what I want!" She jumped up.

"Where are you going?" asked Deborah.

"My parents, my poor parents!" Stephanie exclaimed. "I have made them suffer over and over for years!"

"Stephanie, come and sit down, let's talk this through." Deborah held Stephanie's arm to encourage her to sit. "Take a deep breath. If you go rushing to anyone with this, they will lock you up in the loony bin for sure."

"Okay, you're right, oh my gosh I feel like a huge weight just came off my shoulders. What just happened?"

"I don't know, but your whole face just changed. Whatever it is let's hang out here for a while and get used to it before anyone tries to talk you out of it. Just let it sink in, sit with it for a moment."

Deborah and Stephanie sat for a while trying to take in what just happened. Deborah thought about all the times she had used her story to get a guy to feel sorry for her or another woman to be impressed with how she had coped. "I just had a thought," reflected Deborah. "You and I could compete in the World's Worst Tragedy Championships!" They both fell about laughing again.

"Oh this feels good!" breathed Stephanie.

"What does?"

"I dunno, laughing, letting go, getting real, all of it I guess?" confessed Stephanie smiling. "Thank you."

"I didn't do anything!" answered Deborah.

"But that's the point I think, you didn't want to fix me or do what they always want me to do, to go back over it all again and again and make myself miserable again. I can see a way out now... I think it's time to take off my child abuse crown and resign."

The two young women hugged as Stephanie got up to go and Deborah thanked her for her courage and willingness to grow.

Deborah was so excited to see Stephanie again. To help someone have a breakthrough like this was exhilarating. She told Shelly all about it, and Shelly advised her to go slowly and keep her feet on the ground.

"It's like she just arrived in a new country and she needs to get used to the climate before she goes off exploring on her own. I've had people have breakthroughs like this and then the family and the therapist freak out, which makes the client nuts and you are back to square one again."

At the next session, Stephanie was still on a high. She had so much to say that Deborah just needed to listen.

"I see now how much I made my poor parents pay for what happened to me. I always knew they didn't know it was happening but I've been so angry that they didn't know. I told myself they didn't care enough, and that's why they didn't know, I mean if they loved me enough then it wouldn't have happened, but it really wasn't their fault."

"You know it was a big eye-opener for me to realize how angry I was after my attack," explained Deborah. "I was this ball of emotions, and I didn't know that a lot of it was anger. In fact, it wasn't until a few years later I realized that I wasn't actually angry at the men who attacked me, they didn't know who I was so it wasn't personal, but I was angry that they didn't leave me any scars."

"What?" exclaimed Stephanie, caught by surprise.

"Well, I was so hurt by the injustice of it, so deeply shocked and terrified but I didn't have any lasting scars to explain the pain I was in. My face and hands were all cut up, my ears were bloody and swollen because they kicked me in the head so much but those healed in a week or two and no one could see the broken ribs and concussion. So as soon as the scars went away, so did the sympathy and attention, but I was still hurting. Viktor Frankl says it's not just the physical pain which hurts the most... *'It is the mental agony caused by the injustice, the unreasonableness of it all.'* [1]"

Stephanie thought for a while, tears welling up in her eyes. "Yes, I was just a little kid, I couldn't defend myself, and the very people who were supposed to look after me didn't, that's what hurt so much. But I'm beginning to see that my parents really didn't know. They trusted Su Li Ann to take care of me. I have made their lives miserable punishing them for something that wasn't their fault. How am I ever going to say sorry?"

Deborah took her hand. "I haven't met your parents, but I'm sure they just want you to be happy and safe. You can tell them what you have realized and that you are sorry for punishing them and then they will do with that what they choose. The voice inside your head that tells you that you are responsible for their reaction is a liar, don't listen to it. I think the main thing for you is to forgive them for not knowing and to forgive yourself for not knowing any better, too. And once you forgive everyone, you can put it all behind you and move on. You are not your abuse, you never were, and now you know it."

"I have held them guilty for too long," admitted Stephanie. "There is nothing to forgive."

Around this time Shelly had two more clients for Deborah to talk to. "You seem to be doing so well with Stephanie I thought I could give you some more. Are you up to it?"

Deborah knew that Shelly was swamped with new clients and fundraising, so she smiled and asked for the details. "Okay, thank you. So this one is Fran, her son severely injured a small child while drunk driving."

"Yikes!"

"Yes, it was terrible. Her son is 21 and ran over a five-year-old. The child needed surgery and is going to have trouble walking, and her son's in a detention center now waiting for trial, but she is suffering terribly and needs our help."

"Okay, and the other?"

"Another child abuse case I'm afraid... Angela."

"It was raining as she walked to the Crisis Center to meet Angela. Deborah was getting more confident every time she met with someone or did a shift on the hotline, and Shelly was right, every time she explained to someone that the answers were within and that they can be as strong and resilient as they want, she felt stronger herself. Angela, just 18 was pacing up and down in the hallway when Deborah arrived.

"Are you the shrink?" demanded Angela in her

North London accent.

"No, I'm not a shrink, I'm a volunteer counsellor," corrected Deborah with a big smile.

"Yeah whatever, that's what I mean. I've been waiting," scolded Angela.

"Okay, let's go in here, and we can get started."

They went into one of the counseling rooms and sat across from each other in the armchairs.

"So how does this work? Do you ask me questions or do I tell you what happened? I have never done this before, so I don't know how it works. I've seen a few movies where the patient just cries and cries and then the shrink says time up, or the patient lies on the bed, and just talks and the therapist takes a ton of money for the privilege. I'm not stupid, in fact, I'm not sure why I'm here, it's all just a big mess, and if I don't do something about it, then there will just be more trouble."

Angela took a breath and Deborah jumped in to try and answer one of her many questions.

"So first of all, you are not a patient here. Maybe a client but that's not important. You can tell me what happened if you like, it seems like a good place to start if you are ready?"

Angela chewed on her lip for a moment, hesitating. "Well, he touched me where he shouldn't have, didn't he."

"Who did?" inquired Deborah gently.

Angela looked up and down and up again but couldn't or wouldn't reply.

"It's okay, you are safe here. You don't have to tell me, and I don't have to tell anyone else if you don't want me to. Take your time." Angela played with her long curly hair for a little while, the battle inside was almost visible on her face. After a long pause, she blurted out "Me stepdad!"

"Oh no, I'm so sorry," gasped Deborah, "I'm so

sorry this happened to you."

"Well, he's going to pay right? They're going to send him away right? Cuz he's going to do it again, I know he is, he's a dirty old beggar!"

Angela was shaking, she had her hands over her eyes as if to hide from the ghastly story.

"When did this happen, Angela?"

"I was little."

"When you were...five or six?"

"Yeah, well no, he married my Mom when I was about 14, so a year after that I guess. I was a real cutie...but that's no excuse right?"

"No, there's no excuse. Does anyone else know?"

"Oh God no. My Mum will die when she finds out!"

"Is there anyone else at home, any brothers or sisters?"

"Yeah, there's Michael and my two sisters, Linda and Donna."

"I have a brother called Michael," ventured Deborah, trying to keep things calm.

"Yeah, well, my Michael is going to beat the living daylights out of me stepdad when he finds out."

"You keep saying when they find out. Are you planning to go to the police?"

"Yeah, well that's why I came here first, I was told you go to the police with us when I make a statement?"

"Yes, we can do that. Can you tell me a little bit more about what happened? I know it's difficult."

Angela hesitated again, her finger all twisted up in her hair. She took her time recanting the many occasions that her stepfather had been inappropriate with her, she didn't give many specifics but was clearly traumatized at the thought of it. Deborah asked Shelly to come in and advise them on what to do next and what to expect if she went ahead and filed a police report. Shelly asked her if she was sure, this was a big step, and maybe she should talk to her mother before going to the police, but Angela was sure it was what she wanted to do, and the three women arranged to meet Sunday morning and go to the police station.

What amazed Deborah is that the whole time they were in Shoreditch Police Station helping Angela, she wasn't at all stressed. The only two other times she had ever been in a police station was to give her own statements, but here she was, quite okay, she hardly even thought about her past experiences. The interview room looked the same, the smells and sounds were the same as the other ones, but she was entirely neutral to it. Her new understanding had simply melted all the hatred she'd had for that police detective. It had just slipped away without her having to do anything. She held Angela's hand and stayed present and neutral throughout the whole thing.

8
Leicester Square

1993

As the build for The Flintstones continued, the crew was becoming a tight-knit group. Everyone was excited to be working on this amazing project, and Deborah was feeling very grateful to be included. A new movie called *The Piano* had just come out, and they all decided to go and see it. It was fun to all leave work together and take the Tube into town to Leicester Square and have a night out together. The thought of going down into the Tube station had been terrifying not too long ago, but Deborah was doing really well. Any thoughts of danger were pushed out of her head, it had become automatic to ignore anything she didn't want to think about. Deborah had always loved costume dramas and had been looking forward to this one, but later when they were coming out of the theater, she realized she was filled with extreme feelings and not good ones.

"That was great!" announced Sue as she lit up a cigarette.

"Yeah, I loved it," agreed Larry joining in. "Right, Deborah?"

"I hated it." Deborah was shocked at herself for having such a strong reaction.

"What!!" cried Sue, "it was so good!"

"Really? I just wanted to slap her," said Deborah, incredulously.

"What are you talking about, Debs? It was the 1800s! Women had no voice then so she took control of the one thing she had, her own voice."

"Right, she chose to have no voice?"

"But that's the point!" pleaded Sue. "No one was listening to her."

"Well I wanted to slap her for being a selfish cow," replied Deborah. "She couldn't get her own way, so she had a tantrum, a tantrum that affected a lot of people including her own daughter! If she really wanted to make a difference, she could have worked for it. Plenty of women did in those days like Florence Nightingale and Marie Curie. Instead, she acted like a petulant child."

"Uh, ok," interrupted Larry, "Let's get a drink?"

Sue started laughing. "I love how a group of people can see the same movie and have a completely different experience of it."

Deborah's reaction had taken away any desire to hang out. "It's ok, I'm going home. I'm tired, see you guys tomorrow."

"Uh, I'll come with you," said Larry. "I'm kind of tired myself."

As Larry walked with her to the Underground Station, he started to tell her he was really interested in her, that he had been thinking about her for a while and then out of the blue just before they were about to walk down the steps of the Underground Station he asked her out for a date! Deborah was quite taken aback.

"Uh...thanks, Larry. I'm very flattered, but I don't think so." She tried to think of an excuse that wouldn't hurt his feelings. "I just want to concentrate on work right now, tonight was great, but I just want to be friends."

Larry was clearly disappointed, he had been working up to this for a while but said okay, and they parted.

Sue couldn't stop laughing the next morning at work when Deborah told her about the embarrassing story of Larry asking her out. "He's so much older, and he barely comes up to your elbow!"

"I know! It was so awkward, what was he thinking?" squealed Deborah.

"Don't worry about it, take it as a compliment, he's probably got a Napoleon complex or something," replied Sue, puffing on her cigarette.

Deborah shivered at the thought of it and went back to work.

Sue and the other heads of the departments soon flew out to LA to start filming *The Flintstones* for a three-month shoot, and Deborah was kept on to work on some smaller projects in London. She made a gorilla for a Weetabix commercial, a recreation of King Kong with the arm of the gorilla coming in to take Faye Ray's breakfast cereal instead of her. She got to go on set with her puppet and spent two fun days shooting the commercial. It was quirky and not meant to fool anyone, but Deborah was learning so much about filming and production. She couldn't believe how her life was turning around.

The next class at The Center was intriguing. Francesca had just bought a new book and was very excited to talk about it. She held it up, *Return to Love*. The cover, which glowed in shades of lavender, was a photograph of an attractive woman resting her chin on her folded hands. "This is Marianne Williamson and her new book, it's impressive. I met her when I was in

New York, and she is such an incredible woman. Her book is a triumph, and I highly recommend you all read it. In fact, I want to read a few things out here tonight, and then I thought we could discuss them:

> Our deepest fear is not that we are inadequate. Our deepest fear is that we are powerful beyond measure. It is our light, not our darkness that most frightens us. We ask ourselves, who am I to be brilliant, gorgeous, talented, fabulous? Actually, who are you not to be? You are a child of God. Your playing small does not serve the world. There is nothing enlightened about shrinking so that other people won't feel insecure around you. We are all meant to shine as children do. We are born to make manifest the glory of God that is within us. It's not just in some of us, it's in everyone, and as we let our own light shine, we unconsciously give other people permission to do the same. As we are liberated from our own fear, our presence automatically liberates others." [1]

The group sat silently soaking up the inspirational words that seemed to hover in the air with hope and light.

"You see, ladies, you all have your own journey of how you came to be here. You have grown and escaped that place of suffering, and that is what is going to inspire the women you work with that they can do the same."

"Wow!" gasped Nicola. "I am blown away. When I came here to get help for my agoraphobia following the King's Cross Tube fire. I thought I would be living alone in darkness for the rest of my life and now I see...that there was a...a purpose to it all."

"Oh my gosh, I know this is tacky, but I was afraid you were going to say that you see the light at the end of the tunnel, you know, an Underground Tunnel!" said Susie shaking her head and flapping her hands in front of her face.

They all burst out laughing. Deborah loved the laughing, it was real and spontaneous, like when she had laughed with Stephanie. For so long she had done nothing but cry.

"Yes," agreed Francesca, "seeing purpose in what you have been through is a huge insight, as she says, 'the miracle is the change inside our minds and hearts."

"But what if someone doesn't believe in God?" asked Andrea.

"Like me." Added Deborah who was feeling a bit uncomfortable about the whole God thing.

"Ok, well I'm not sure I do either," confessed Francesca. "At least not in a religious way. In fact, I think what Marianne would say is that we can all have our own way of believing in God. Religious people seem to think of him as an old man sitting on a throne up in heaven, some see him as a kindly grandfather figure, others see him as a tyrannical master dishing out justice and punishment, and others from eastern religions see God as a Divine Essence that is within us all. I think what is important is that you have an understanding that works for you. I would encourage any of you to come up with your own ideas of God if the conventional ones don't work."

"But that would be like Frankenstein," refuted

Deborah. "You can't make up your own God. God can't be something that you make up or trade in for a newer model like a car - Ooh I think I will get leather seats this time! Uh, a God who will give me lots of money and Brad Pitt to marry. That gives me the power, and that would make me God?!"

"Lord help us!" cried Susie.

"Right," continued Francesca, "but listen carefully. I'm not suggesting you make up your own God, I'm suggesting you can have your own understanding, of the relationship you have with God. Can you see the difference? You don't even have to call it God, you can call it whatever you want."

Deborah wasn't sure, she knew what believing in God had done for the Jews in Europe and the suffering in the Middle Ages as Catholicism had put the world in servitude to Rome, she didn't even want to think about it.

"Look, here at The Center we aren't saying we believe or don't believe, we are open and supportive to what our clients need and if they are open to talking about a loving Energy if you like, bigger than themselves or even inside of themselves and it helps them, then that's good. The last thing I want is for you to think I'm pushing some kind of religion or even a spiritual thing here. It's just about being open-minded to all ideas, that's all."

"Shelly, do you believe in God?" asked Deborah later that week.

"I believe in a loving Power, a Divine Source of everything that I don't understand," She was washing the dishes in her kitchen "Why? What brought that up?"

"Oh, it was just something Francesca said. She read something in class; it was really inspiring, but it had a lot of God in it."

Shelly laughed. "She read from her new favorite book?"

"Yep."

"Marianne Williamson is Jewish, did you know that?"

"Really? But she's from Texas!"

Shelly laughed again. "We Jews get everywhere! Besides, I think her middle name is Deborah. So what bothers you so much about this God stuff?"

"Well I have always seen it as weak I guess, like believing in fairy tales."

"Okay, I could see that. Fairy tales are childish, but what if God was real?"

Deborah looked at her as if to say, are you for real?

"Okay like this. Think about someone we both know. Sue for example. Let's say I understand her as a black man from Chicago? Now that might hinder my relationship with Sue, but it wouldn't change the essential facts of who Sue is. You understand her as a white woman from North London, so your relationship with her is probably going to be more successful, but she is still Sue no matter what either of us think about her. That's how I understand God. I have my thoughts, Hymie has his, the Rabbi has his, and I'm sure the Archbishop of Canterbury has his understanding of God too, but that doesn't change who God is. Could you see that?"

Deborah was quiet for a bit. "I think I need to think about this one."

"How about this," offered Shelly. "Could you see that there is a spooky spiritual Wisdom that guides us, that everyone has it? Problem is that it gets covered up by all that over-thinking and misunderstanding that distresses us and distracts us from the deep truth that is always inside of us. For me, it's the sparkle in people's eyes. That's their soul shining through, and people who are awake to that just...sparkle."

"Maybe," Deborah was still on the fence. "I still don't see why you have to call it *God*."

"That's okay. Maybe for you, it's not? I think Francesca was just trying to respect others who feel that it is, that's all. Now dry these, and we can have a nice cup of tea."

About three weeks after Sue and the crew had left for LA, the "big boss" at the London workshop called Deborah into his office. She was nervous. She knew the job she'd been hired for was over, so she guessed he was saying goodbye till next time.

"We love the work you did on *Flintstones*," announced Jim, "but I need you to go to LA."

Deborah's heart jumped. "We just got awarded another movie, and I need to bring back the main crew to start doing R&D for it, so I need to send you out there to supervise the creatures for the rest of filming. They have it all set up, and I'm leaving a mechanic and a computer guy there so you'll have everything you need. They are shooting somewhere in North L.A. called Sunshine Valley. Can you leave...on Thursday?"

Deborah stared at him. She couldn't quite process what was happening. He was bringing six experienced people back and sending her to L.A. instead for three months of filming. "Sure," she stuttered, almost having an out of body experience. "Thanks! I think..."

9
North Hollywood

Deborah stood in line at Heathrow waiting to check in for her Virgin Atlantic flight to LA. She was very nervous. Not nervous about flying, that was always exciting but worried about the tickets and her passport. Maybe they didn't have her in the computer? Why was it taking so long? Did she pack the right clothes? There was so much she didn't know. The line of passengers and suitcases snaked around the Virgin red ropes, but it just wasn't moving. She rechecked her passport and wondered how it would be in California. What if the production assistant wasn't there to pick her up at LAX? How would she get to the hotel? They had been standing in line for ages, and she could see the staff were buzzing around trying to take care of something. Everyone else seemed to be traveling with someone, and so had someone to commiserate with. She felt alone and wondered what the problem was. Finally, a very smiley blonde lady in her bright red Virgin outfit came along the line handing out a piece of paper. It was a letter from Richard Branson!

"Ooh look at that," exclaimed the lady in front of Deborah, "Richard Branson says he's sorry we have had to wait! Awh isn't that nice of him and him being so busy."

"Don't be daft luv, he didn't write out 200 letters by hand!" said her husband, and then finally, to everyone's relief, the line started to move.

Sunshine Valley, California sounded so exotic when Deborah was sitting in the cold, old Victorian workshop in London, but it was actually a disused quarry at the other end, the really far other end, of Lankershim Boulevard in North Hollywood. American streets are so long. English streets might get up to 121 in numbers but the street addresses in LA were like 8151, and Lankershim Boulevard went on forever. And it was hot. No shortage of sunshine here. Driving an automatic for the first time, and on the other side of the road, was enough to stress anyone out, let alone the onslaught of culture, language and a new city to navigate. The first obstacle Deborah needed to navigate was the hotel dining room. Everything was different. Just having a cup of tea for breakfast the first day was a challenge. There was coffee everywhere, so she asked for tea, only to be presented with a very sad looking tea bag on a saucer. She was then presented with two small metal jugs, one containing lukewarm water and the other some greasy white stuff she later found out was called half and half. The warm water did its best to leach some flavour out of the sad-looking tea bag, but the greasy white stuff just put the nail in the coffin of the having a cup of tea idea, and she opted for orange juice instead.

Sue had stayed on for a few days to show her around but soon she was gone, leaving behind her a welcome stash of British tea bags. The pressure at work to get it right and look like she knew what she was doing felt almost as heavy as the massive dinosaurs she was about to take care of.

The first job she had to do was repair the T-Rex that was going to be holding Elizabeth Taylor in its mouth the next day. Apparently, it had a big tear in the latex skin on its nose. The first A.D. had told her it was on an empty soundstage at Universal Studios, so she went over to stage 27 to see what could be done. As she walked into the stale air of the cavernous film studio, she could see a massive decapitated T-Rex head lying on its side. But that wasn't the scary part. About eight men were standing around waiting for her. These men were seasoned special effects guys. Tough guys, the kind of guys who do rigging, explosions, and car crashes, physical effects that make you believe and feel as if an earthquake is actually happening. They had just come off a new movie called Jurassic Park, and Deborah had heard rumours it was going to be a big hit. Michael Lantieri, an award-winning special effects giant who worked with Henson's American competitor, Stan Winston, had brought his crew to watch her, the 'expert who was just flown in from London,' heal this wounded monster.

Deborah was determined to keep her cool. She was just 28 years old, her first time on a movie set, her first time in the United States. She had never even seen this puppet before, she had no idea what to do, and to top it off, she was being scrutinized by eight seasoned professional older men. "*Focus,*" Deborah said to herself sternly. "*Focus!*"

Her colleagues had left behind a box of supplies, so she rummaged through to see what was there. She found some latex scraps, some contact adhesive, some sandpaper, and some talcum powder. There were some paints and some scissors. Deborah suddenly felt a surge of gratitude to her father. When she was young, he had taught her how to fix a puncture in her bicycle tire. She had watched her father mend it with a patch of latex rubber, and he used contact adhesive! She took a deep breath and sanded down the area around the tear to make the contact adhesive stick better. She cut a piece of latex the right shape and texture for the patch and applied glue to the nose and the patch - the glue was tacky almost instantly in the heat of the soundstage - and then she pressed it on praying for it to work. It looked promising, so she used the talcum powder to get off any stickiness and then painted it to blend it in with the original skin. Phew!

The men just stood and watched. Apart from a few introductions, they hadn't said much, and now she was done. She stepped back and put the supplies back in the box.

"That's the first nose job I've seen up close," said one of the guys as they congratulated her and thanked her for letting them watch. Deborah felt faint but smiled as she said some goodbyes, hoping no one could hear her heart thumping. She could hardly sleep that night, worried sick that it would peel off overnight and that she would be shouted at in front of the whole crew and let her boss and Sue down. As she lay there, her thoughts wandered around, and she thought about her conversations with Shelly back in London and wondered how Stephanie and Angela were doing. There was no internet, no cell phones, not even pagers yet, and an international call was not in the budget for such a silly thing. She tossed and turned in her hotel bed and finally gave up and got up to watch something called cable TV.

The day before, the production office had sent round a note to the crew asking them to be on their best behaviour when Ms. Taylor was on set. Elizabeth Taylor was Hollywood royalty, and she was playing Fred Flintstone's mother-in-law. The next day, the whole crew, the camera, lighting, and prop guys even the transport guys and caterers all wore ties out of respect. They still had their T-shirts, shorts, and work boots on, but each man wore a tie in honour of Ms.

Taylor's visit. She was very touched. The T-Rex had been moved out to the quarry overnight where they were about to film Liz in its mouth, but because Elizabeth Taylor was the Queen of Hollywood and not as young as she once was, they had put the dinosaur head on its side so she could comfortably stand upright. The camera was also tilted on its side, but in the editing room they would turn it all back upright to give the impression that she was dangling in its mouth. Deborah was learning that the world of special effects is all about fooling the audience into believing things that aren't real, really are, or things that couldn't possibly happen, like Liz being picked up in the mouth of a T-Rex, really could happen.

Deborah parked her rental car in the crew parking lot and walked straight over to sneak a peek at her work. She had that sick feeling in her stomach, and she had the "thought police" on standby as she walked across the Bedrock film set, but felt reassured as she couldn't hear any shouting. Everyone was eating at the breakfast truck, and nothing had really happened yet, so she was able to take a quick look.

"So where was it ripped?" asked the 1st A.D., popping up from nowhere.

Deborah grinned. "If you can't tell, then I must have done a good job!" She felt glorious like she did that day her teacher held up one of her paintings in class when she was seven years old. With the energy that comes from great relief she turned and almost skipped to get herself her new favorite discovery, a breakfast burrito.

Filming with the animatronic puppets put her right in the middle of the action. First, she had to set up the puppet ready for the scene like any other actor who needed to be on their spot ready for the director's cue. Just before each take, she would place a tiny drop of silicone oil in its eyes to make it catch the light like a real eye does, fluff the feathers just right, and dart out the way when the director shouted *Action!* She was its hair and makeup artist, bodyguard, and doctor all rolled into one. After three months of many more first-time experiences, compliments, and well-covered-up mistakes, filming was over, and she returned to London, triumphant. She had worked with Steven Spielberg, met Michael Jackson when he came to visit Liz Taylor and had lunch with one of her favourite bands, The B-52's, who were making a cameo appearance in the movie. Walking back into the workshop in North London she felt like a star, but after a few hellos and how was its, she was back at work on the next project. This time it was dogs. She and Sue were going to make copies of Australian sheepdogs for a little low-budget movie called *Babe*.

Babe was set in the English countryside. It is so quintessentially English that it was weird to hear that this movie was going to be shot in Australia.

"Well, that's Hollywood for you," Norman told her. "An Aussie production company has bought the rights, so they are making a corner of New South Wales look like a Somerset farm!"

The six-month build was going to be tough but exciting. No one had ever done this standard of animatronic work before. Getting the dogs exactly right almost seemed like an impossible task. They were working from photographs taken by a P.A. in Australia, so it was challenging to see the details in the black-and-white fur. An Australian sheepdog was brought in from a dog kennel in the Suburbs for them to get a better idea, but these puppets had to be exact copies of the dogs in Australia chosen to act in the movie, so it was quite a challenge. Sue taught Deborah more skills and techniques, and together with the mechanics, computer guys, and fabricators, they made eight amazing, lifelike animatronic dogs. The story called for a male and female, Rex and Fly, and each one needed a sitting, lying, standing, and floppy version with two interchangeable heads each. It was a lot of intense, detailed work. The hair on the dogs' faces needed to be put in one at a time, delicately following the intricate direction of hair on a real dog. Deborah was loving it.

The day finally came when Norman confirmed the crew for Australia: Deborah, Sue, Larry, Mitch, and ten others were going Down Under for six months of filming.

"Six months!" exclaimed Mitch. "My cat will forget all about me."

"My kids will forget about me!" laughed Sue.

As for Deborah, she was ecstatic.

10
Sydney

1994

It still struck Deborah as kind of strange that they had flown thousands of miles to the other side of the world to make a movie that was set back home in England, but hey, that was Hollywood for you. They were working in the business of illusions, so why not? It was also strange to have flown thousands of miles to find a country that had the Queen on the money and to hear the locals talking about cricket and drinking tea. Australia was beautiful, the weather was always just right, and the grey-and-pink parrots that sat in the trees outside Deborah's hotel window made it just perfect. For the first few days, they stayed in Sydney, while the production office sorted out houses, apartments, and rental cars for the crew out in the small Bush town where they would be living for the next six months. Deborah was exhausted after two very long flights. It had taken almost twenty-four hours of flying to get from London to Sydney, and now she was just happy to be out in the fresh air. As she walked through the hotel lobby to the dining room, she could see there was a commotion going on by the front door.

"I asked you to call the police, please do as I ask and call the police!" demanded Larry sternly to the concierge. "It's not where I left it so obviously it's been stolen, call the police, now!"

"What's been stolen?" whispered Deborah to Sue who was watching the show unfold.

"Larry's rental car has been stolen," said Sue.

"Yikes," exclaimed Deborah. "He's he's only had it a couple of hours!"

"I only left it there for a minute!" yelled Larry, pointing to the driveway just to the left of the main entrance.

The staff were doing their best to keep Larry calm, so Deborah and Sue went into the dining room for some supper. It was nice to have a proper meal and take advantage of the time to relax. They knew that as soon as the crates with all their work and supplies arrived tomorrow, it would be full speed ahead for months. As they walked back through the lobby after their meal, they saw that the commotion was still going on.

"So typical of Larry! Let's see what's happening now," said Sue.

The sun had gone down, but it was still warm as they walked outside to the driveway to see what everyone was looking at. To the left of the main entrance was a large natural pond surrounded by reeds and ornamental trees, and through the murky water were two beams of light.

"Oh no!" laughed Sue. "They stole his car and drove it into the pond!"

"No," corrected a hotel worker, "he didn't put it into park, and it drifted there by itself!"

"You're kidding me?!" exclaimed Deborah, trying not to laugh.

"Apparently he had never driven an automatic before and didn't know that once you stop, you need to put it into park," said the hotel guy. "You Pommies are a liability!"

"How are they going to get it out?"

"A tow truck is on its way, but it's a write-off,"

replied the hotel guy.

Sue and Deborah had a good laugh, but Larry was gone.

The next day was a big one. After months of building the animatronic puppets, it was time to introduce them to the real animals who would be acting the parts where running and walking was needed. Sue and Deborah were a bit nervous, as the Director and Producer - in fact, anyone who was around - came to watch the unveiling. The real dogs were being put through their paces by the head animal trainer, who then called them to stand next to their fake colleagues. Everyone was astounded by how accurate the puppets were. The size, the shape, the hair colour of the animatronic dogs. Everything was almost identical.

"Phew, that's a relief!" gasped Sue.

Everyone complimented the two women on their work, but they were all surprised that the real dogs weren't interested at all.

Sue cried out, "Oh no! They don't like them?"

"Don't worry," said the animal trainer, "animals are only interested in smell. Your puppets don't smell like real dogs, they smell of glue and latex. You can't fool them, animals are much smarter."

"Wow, that's so interesting," observed Deborah. "We have spent months trying to recreate them, and they're not fooled for a second."

"Don't worry dear, it's just me and the audience you have to convince," said the Director, "and you have done a pretty good job so far. Let's hope it comes out this good on film. We are doing a film test later I think."

"Thanks!"

The Production Office had been installed in a girls school that had been vacated a few years earlier. Sue and Deborah were given an upper classroom as a workshop. The rest of the animatronics crew was down in what had been the auditorium, and the gym had been made into a screening room. The next day, Deborah ventured in to watch the screen tests. The windows had been blacked out with bin bags, and the Director, Producers, and various crew members were standing around watching the footage from the day before. Deborah moved to the back where she always felt more comfortable and found herself standing next to a charming looking gentleman.

"Tall ones in the back," he whispered to her with a smile. Deborah smiled back as she watched the various tests being projected on the wall. As they went through the actors' makeup tests, she realised that the man standing next to her was the actor playing the farmer! She looked at him out of the corner of her eye just to make sure.

"Hi, I'm Jamie," he whispered.

"Hi, nice to meet you, Farmer Hoggett," whispered Deborah, with a big smile.

Next, it was the dogs' turn.

"So, what do you do in this circus?" inquired Jamie quietly.

"I worked on the dogs."

"You're an animal trainer?"

Deborah stifled a laugh, "No, I work for Henson's, those aren't real, they are puppets."

"Wow!" exclaimed Jamie covering his mouth, "you guys are good! I thought I was looking at the real animals!"

"Thanks," replied Deborah with a relieved grin. "That's our job, to convince you that they are real."

Jamie smothered a laugh. "My mind does that to me all the time!"

Down the hall from Sue and Deborah in the next classroom was the Editing Suite. Everything was temporary and makeshift, and as soon as filming started, the editor was busy making the first cuts. Deborah found it fascinating to watch him at work on the new state-of-the-art Avid digital editing system. Gone were the days of film all over the floor and scissors and Scotch tape. Sharing the editing room was the Visual Effects Supervisor, Steve, an American who Deborah soon realised was in charge of all the Visual Effects on the film, not just the computer effects that would be added later, but her work too. She figured out that that kind of made him her boss, so she decided it would be good to get to know him; besides, he was kind of cute.

As the weeks went on, Steve would pass by and sometimes stick his head around the door to say hi, and soon he was stopping by regularly for a chat. He was from Boston but lived in San Francisco. Steve had gone to an Ivy League school and then been headhunted by George Lucas to work at his Skywalker Ranch facility in Northern California, where he had designed some Oscar-winning computer graphics work. He was now freelance, and this was his first big movie as a Visual Effects Supervisor. He had the massive job of filming and logging all the shots that would be later enhanced with computer graphics back in Los Angeles in post-production, it was an enormous responsibility.

Soon it was time for the dogs to be on set and Steve was really helpful in getting the shots just right. By now they were hanging out together all the time, and the friendship flourished. Steve told Deborah how much he liked her ideas and they talked endlessly about work and movies, people and life.

About six weeks before the end of the six-month film shoot, disaster struck. Deborah woke up at about 4 a.m. in agony, her neck rigid with her chin fixed down onto her right collarbone. The pain was off the charts, she thought maybe a hot shower would help relax the muscles, but she could barely keep from screaming. She called Sue to say what had happened and that she wouldn't be in and waited in excruciating pain till 9 a.m. for the local chiropractor in the next village to open its doors. She couldn't drive as she couldn't move her head, so she limped along the Australian bush dirt track to the Chiropractor's clinic. She just managed to push open the door of the waiting room when the receptionist saw her and jumped up.

"You're as white as a ghost my love, come and sit down." Everyone fussed over her, the doctor said they needed an X-ray to see what happened and so Deborah followed him into the surgery, where he positioned her standing up against the X-ray wall.

"Can you stand up straight for me, Sweetheart?" he asked.

"I can't!" She was exhausted, on the edge of tears, and ready to fall over.

After the X-ray, she lay down to rest until the chiropractor came back with the results. Out the window, she could just see a eucalyptus tree where four, maybe five pink-and-grey parrots were perched, looking in.

"Did you know your neck was broken?" inquired the Chiropractor, as he came back into the room.

"No?" Deborah was completely thrown by his question. Did he just ask that? What did it mean? Was she going to be in a wheelchair or something? She tried not to panic.

"Did you have some kind of blunt-force collision, a car accident maybe?"

Deborah flashed back to the sixteen-year-old boy who had thrown the bike at her in London and how she couldn't lift her head the next day. Her thoughts were steady, but she could feel her heart speeding up as the memories came flooding back.

"Yes...a kid attacked me...he threw a bike at my head while I was riding...but that was two years ago?"

"The body is an amazing thing," explained the doctor. "Your body has held it together all this time, but now it needs some help. See here, C2 and C3 are cracked." He pointed at the X-ray, but Deborah couldn't make out anything in the grey-and-black shadows. "You need to rest and take it easy and let me help get movement back in that neck of yours." said the doctor, kindly.

"But I have to get back to work!" cried Deborah, worried about Sue and the rest of the crew. There was still a month left of filming. It wasn't registering with her that she needed to stop and take care of herself. The work ethic that had been drilled into her by her parents and being self-employed had forced her into always putting her job first. It wasn't like an office job where the papers would still be on a desk next week. The puppets were like actors, and they needed her on set! She felt responsible, there was no taking time off to rest!

She finally agreed to take two days off, and then it would be the weekend. The doctor found a ride from a neighbor to take Deborah home, there wasn't much he could do that first day; she screamed if he even tried to touch her. Later that day, Steve brought her soup, which they discovered was quite challenging to eat lying on the floor, so he rummaged around to find a straw.

On Monday morning, she walked cautiously into the workshop feeling very shaky and unsteady. Everyone kind of ignored her and she almost felt invisible. Strange, she thought to herself, what's up with that? She explained to Norman that she would need to see the doctor regularly, but she would take late appointments after shooting so as not to interfere with work too much. A couple of days went by, and she noticed that the animatronics crew were being very cold to her, no one asked how she was doing or what had happened, it was quite weird. She felt betrayed almost, she was taking a risk by not resting and felt hurt by their coldness. She asked Sue if she had heard anything, but she hadn't so she decided to ignore it. The Doctor saw her every other day for the first week, and then twice a week, and then once a week until he managed to get full movement back into her neck. He was a gentle, kind family man who took really good care of her, even coming in on his days off to give her treatments and Steve did his best to help her and made sure she had what she needed.

The following week after the neck incident, one of the mechanics got the flu. He was off all week, and the crew had a whip-round to buy him some balloons and a card. Deborah was flabbergasted, she had a broken neck, and she didn't even get a "hi how are you"? She knew something wasn't right, it just didn't make sense, and then the next day as she was walking through the main workshop, her boss laid into her.

"Are you off loafing again?" accused Norman suddenly.

"No?" replied Deborah quite taken aback, "I'm just getting some pliers to fix the claws on the female dog."

"It's about time you pulled your weight around here!" Norman shouted angrily. Deborah was shocked, what on earth was he talking about? "You haven't been working as part of this team for a while now, and we didn't bring you all this way just to goof off!"

Deborah was speechless. Everyone had turned around and were staring at her, she wanted the ground to open up and swallow her. Her heart was pounding, and she felt her face flush with humiliation. Norman walked away before she could say anything, so she turned and walked straight out and back up to her workroom. She wanted to cry, she wanted to run, she wanted Steve, but he was in a meeting with the Director, and Sue wasn't anywhere to be seen.

That night she told Steve what had happened, how no one had stood up for her. Steve didn't understand either, he was infuriated that they would treat her that way.

"It reminded me of when I was about six years old on my first day of school. They were calling all the names of all the kids to go to their classrooms, and I was left behind. It was so humiliating, I thought I was going to die of shame." Then just like that in the flash of a thought, Deborah realised something. "Oh my... I can't believe it!"

"What?" uttered Steve.

"It was alphabetical!!"

"What was?"

"The roll call! On the first day of school!! They were calling the kids by their last names! I'm an S. Don't you see?"

Steve looked confused, what was she talking about now?

"I'm an S, so I was at the end of the list of names!

There weren't any kids with last names beginning with X, Y, or Z in my school in 1972! All this time I thought they had forgotten about me! Every time I would remember that first day of school it would bring up all these painful memories and it wasn't even true, it was alphabetical!"

Deborah calmed down, and Steve said he would try to get to the bottom of what was happening at work, but Deborah asked him to let it go.

"We only have a few weeks left," Deborah said with resignation, "and if that's the way they want to be, then let them."

The next few weeks were painful both at work and with her neck, but she kept going and finally got through to the last day of shooting. The rest of the film crew, the electricians, and the camera guys were the same old friendly group of Aussies as they'd always been, and at the end of the last day of shooting, the Director and Producers thanked everyone for their hard work. The animatronics crew who had treated her so badly all went out for a last dinner and booze up, but Deborah had no desire to hang out with them, so she went with Steve, Jamie the actor, and his wife, who'd come for a visit, to a restaurant in the neighboring beach town of Wollongong for a goodbye meal.

The next day, as they were starting the big job of packing up all the supplies and creatures, Mitch the computer whiz kid came to see her.

"Hi," said Mitch sheepishly.

"Hi," replied Deborah a little surprised. They had been good friends and wondered what he wanted.

"I thought you should know something."

"Really, what's that?" said Deborah casually, as she continued to pack their tools and personal things

"Well... I'm pretty sure it was Larry."

"What was?" Deborah didn't look up but continued to work.

"I think he told Norman that those days you took off for your neck...you were at the beach with Steve."

"What?!" demanded Deborah, looking up at him in total disbelief. Her mind went blank for what seemed like ages as she tried to process what Mitch had just said. Her heart was pounding as her mind and body went into overdrive trying to process the cascade of reactions to what she had just heard. She took a deep breath as she tried to put the sudden confusion in her head into words. Then she burst out, "Forget that it's not remotely true, Steve was on set, and I have a doctor's note! I was lying on the floor in agony with a broken neck!!"

Mitch sat down on one of the crates. "Larry has been building a case against you for months, and I think Norman and the rest of the guys had had enough."

"Enough of what?" cried Deborah.

"Steve. They'd had enough of Steve telling them what to do."

"But that's his job, he's the Visual Effects Supervisor, he's going to make our work look amazing, besides what has that got to do with..." Deborah stopped, it all suddenly fell into place. She felt almost dizzy as she put it all together. She had turned Larry down for a date back in London, and now he was getting his own back!

"That little piece of..." Deborah stopped herself

"Yeah, I know. I'm sorry it had to end like this but they hate Steve, he's the enemy."

"What are you talking about? He's the sweetest guy here!" said Deborah still in disbelief.

"His computer graphics and effects are going to be the end of our kind of work," explained Mitch, "and the guys downstairs are scared for their careers, there aren't going to be many more films like this one. You watch, it's going to be all green screen and computers and CGI in a few years. They won't need our animatronic puppets anymore."

Deborah sat down on another crate and closed her eyes for a minute and took a deep breath.

"He used me because I turned him down for a date, what a little..."

"Larry asked you out?!" asked Mitch laughing in disbelief, "He only comes up to your elbow!"

"*I know!*"

"Wow, what a bad loser, what was he thinking?"

"Loser is right," agreed Deborah, turning back to her packing. "I'm moving to California after this and Larry can go back to his small little world with his very small little thinking and... Oh never mind. I just hope I don't have to see any of them ever again!"

Deborah couldn't wait to be done and get out of there. Her mind was flipping from disbelief to anger and shock. She fought back the tears and as soon as she could, she left to talk it through with Steve. As she drove over to his house, she wanted to scream. She couldn't believe what had happened. Larry had to have told so many lies and kept it up for weeks. But what she couldn't get over was why Norman hadn't asked her for her side of the story?! No wonder they weren't talking to her or asking her how she was! She was a traitor in their eyes, and Larry was the cause of it all. She tried to pull herself together as she drove up the dirt track to the door.

Steve fell silent as Deborah laid it all out for him, and now it was his turn to be in total disbelief, struggling to understand what had happened.

"Wow, that's a whole lot of fear going on there," said Steve, as he sat back in his chair with his hands behind his head, "Do you see?"

He leaned forward. "It's like this. Larry tells himself that he has a chance with you, he creates some fantastical story in his head that it's a possibility and so asking you out makes total sense to him. You say no thanks and his little male ego is flattened, his self-esteem goes through the floor, so what does he do? He looks for an opportunity to punish you and he brings me down too, all to make himself feel better."

"This is why I like talking to you," confessed Deborah, sighing with relief, "but why am I responsible for his self-esteem? For him to even think that asking me out was, okay, I mean, I know I'm not all that but I am so much taller than him and a lot younger, for him to even consider asking me, I'd say his self-esteem was just fine."

"Yes, before," insisted Steve, "but his self-esteem was smashed when you rejected him, and that's why he had to get back at you to build it up again."

"No, I disagree. I don't think self-esteem is something that can go up and down like a yo-yo because of something on the outside. He must've thought there was a possibility I would say yes, and that created a little thought story in his head that made him feel confident enough to ask. I said no, and that started a whole load of insecure thinking, thinking that months, yes months later, he formed into a plan to hurt me."

"Wow, that's pretty twisted!" declared Steve. "So you are saying you think self-esteem is constant?"

"I dunno, I have been trying to work this one out for a while. I think we all have something inside like a soul or something spooky, something pure that can never change or be spoilt but it gets, I dunno...covered up if you like, with negative thinking. It's natural to get insecure when we get hurt or when we think we have been hurt and then we...feel hurt, no? It's just a theory of mine, but I think it's the quality of the thinking that is bouncing up and down from fearful insecurity to narcissistic chutzpah and back again, not the pure self, inner soul, true innocent thing inside, that's constant. He, like most of us, thinks that it's the outside things that need to change for us to feel ok, but it was his thinking that was going up and down, and that's what was causing him to justify revenge. His self-esteem was just fine if he thought he had a right to punish us like some stupid King Baby demanding we are sent to the Tower for not doing what he wants!"

Steve gave her a look as if to say, wow, that was a bit deep, a bit spiritual and then paused for a moment."Yes, but we don't all act like Othello and arrange a plan to wreak revenge and destruction on our enemies!"

"Iago," corrected Deborah.

"What?"

"I think it was Iago who planned the revenge on Othello, not Othello," corrected Deborah, smiling.

"Whatever, Miss 'British education is better than anyone else's.'"

They laughed and started to relax.

"Wow, I totally see how his thinking led to actions that backfired, and now everyone else has to feel bad," continued Steve, shaking his head, "but I still think it was his low self-esteem that made him want revenge."

"Okay, but it was his thinking, the fictitious story he made up in his head that did the lowering. I still think self-esteem is something that is constant, it can't be high or low, go up or down, it's our thinking that changes and that's what affects how we feel. No one who is feeling great ever says, ooh I had better work on my self-esteem in case I lose this great feeling! When we feel great, we are just...in the moment, in touch with our true selves. I'm sure there is something...I don't know, something spooky inside, like wisdom or something real or pure and innocent that can't be touched by outside things. Besides, if he really had low self-esteem, it would make sense to him that I said no and that would have been the end of it. It takes pretty high, if not out-of-control, delusional self-confidence, to plan revenge...as if he thought he was entitled to be treated the way he demanded? I mean, he could have ended our careers!" She paused, and then her thoughts about what happened popped up to the surface again like a cork in water. "Poor Sue. She must have been stuck in the middle of it all. But what I don't get is why Norman and the others didn't ask me if it was true? Some of them had to have seen you on set that day, our stuff is in nearly every shot?"

"Nope, that was the day I was out doing the second-unit shots at the slaughterhouse for the opening scene, remember? That's why I was able to come back early to feed you the soup because we wrapped in the middle of the afternoon."

"Okay, but they didn't even ask? How could they hate us so much? We're all on the same team!"

"First of all, you don't know. Maybe they did ask? Maybe they just asked the wrong people? Like Mitch said, they are scared I'm going to take away their careers," Steve continued, "You of all people should know how specialised this work is. Where else are sculptors and artists like these guys going to get work that takes them around the world and pays silly money? Larry knew exactly how to feed their fears because he is living in a world of fear himself. He knew exactly what to say and how to say it in order to convince them it's true because it's real to him. Larry laid it on gradually, and thick enough so that I was the enemy and our friendship made you a traitor. It's almost like the special effects we do: They believed something that their intelligence could have dismissed if only they'd thought to ask. Being self-employed brings a certain amount of insecurity, and the backstabbing that goes on in this ego-driven business is awful sometimes."

"Are you?" asked Deborah. "Taking our careers away I mean? You know that means me too...?"

"Well...maybe, but not for a long time yet. We are working on a computer program that makes fur look like it's real, like it moves, but your creatures are far more lifelike right now, and that's what we all want to see, right? We all want to be convinced that the cat up there on the screen really can sing and dance, and right now your animatronic creatures are the best way to do that."

Deborah sat back and took in a long sigh. She was so tired of them all, "I'm not worried. It's going to take years for you computer geeks to work out how to do it better than we do. Anyway, I've already decided, I'm not going back to London. The work is in LA, and that's where I'm going. California, here I come."

11
Los Angeles

1994

Deborah had turned thirty while filming in Australia but that all seemed very far away now that she had moved to LA. She had done her best to put what happened Down Under out of her mind, like she had learned to do with all her other uncomfortable thoughts.

The adjustment from London was mostly entertaining, as she observed the differences in culture and language in California. Just driving around with the roof off her little black convertible in the constant sunshine was mesmerising to her. The palm trees and the mountains, the ocean breeze. It was all very seductive. On her first movie since moving to LA, she had made an instant connection with a makeup artist called Abby, who had lived in London for many years and was now back in the States to further her career. Originally from South Carolina, Abby was gracious and generous in helping Deborah get to know her way around. Food shopping, for example, was very confusing with all the different brands and so many choices. In England, she was used to picking up a pint of milk and a loaf of bread, here it was low fat, nonfat, 2%, 10%, and that horrid 'half and half' stuff - it was overwhelming. Even small things were challenging at first, like what an American mailbox looked like. To Deborah, who was used to bright red, elegant British post boxes, the American ones looked very dull, in fact, she had mistaken them for a rubbish bin!

After that first movie finished, Deborah knew she needed to get back into counseling work again. It would keep her feet on the ground and her thoughts under control, especially now that she was mixing with movie stars and famous directors. There were so many egos flying around that it was very hard not to get sucked up into the very competitive game of being successful. Abby had mentioned that there was an Advice Center kind of place in Santa Monica that offered counselling, so she went to check it out. The Santa Monica Drop-in Center, or the SMDC, as it was known, was like the Islington women's Crisis Center but not quite. For a start, there were men. Male counsellors, men's groups, and men who wanted or needed to talk. This struck Deborah as very Californian. The British men she knew would never have set foot in a place like this, or share their feelings with anyone, let alone admit that they had any. Unless it was about football of course.

The SMDC was in a large, old, blue, Californian-style wooden cottage, with hardwood floors and a porch at 2nd and Hill, just a few blocks in from the beach. Built around 1905, Deborah imagined how uncomfortable it must have been for the woman of the house to be wearing a whalebone corset and crinoline in the Californian heat. The four-bedroom house had been turned into an office and counseling rooms. What would have been the parlor was now a large room for 12 Step or therapy groups to hold meetings. She walked up the steps of the porch and opened the screen door and remembered how scared she was when she first stepped into Shelly's office four years earlier. A young man pushed past her on his way out and turned just long enough to point her to the office.

"Ask for Bob," he called, as the screen door

slapped shut behind him. The office door was open, and Deborah glanced inside. Just like Shelly's office, Bob McGowan's office was piled high with papers, filing cabinets, and overflowing ashtrays. What was it about warm-hearted social activist types that made them so untidy, she wondered.

"Come in, sit down, what can I do for you?" offered Bob, as he finished some notes. He closed a manila folder and looked up. He was an older, handsome man with kind, blue eyes, salt-and-pepper hair that was slightly long, and a short goatee beard. She thought to herself that he looked like an actor playing the part.

"I recently moved here from London and…"

"And you thought you would be discovered in the drugstore like Lana Turner but after three weeks you're not a movie star, and now you're depressed?"

"Wow!" said Deborah taken aback, "No, actually I just finished my third movie and I wanted to ask about volunteering. I'm a trained and experienced counsellor!" Deborah was used to having to justify and defend herself on a movie set where she was often the only woman in a crew of thirty men and younger than most of them, but she was surprised to be on the defensive here.

Bob sat back in his chair visibly shocked, "Yikes, I am so sorry. I'm so used to people wanting something for nothing that I've become a little…cynical. I sincerely apologize." He put his hand on his heart to dramatically convey his embarrassment.

"That's okay, I understand," said Deborah, graciously. She told him about her experience and training, and after they had chatted for a while, he suggested that she take a look around and come to their next committee meeting where she could meet the other volunteers.

"Help yourself to coffee. I think the 6 p.m. NA

meeting is starting soon so don't be surprised if there are some junkies in the kitchen, they are usually pretty harmless, and some of them are angels."

Deborah thanked him and took a walk around. There was a notice board in the hallway with a timetable of all the 12-step meetings, group therapy sessions, and other support groups. There was a child abuse survivors group, even a clutterers group. There was a list of services ranging from bereavement counseling to legal aid, all with a sliding scale for payment. She made her way to the kitchen to find two enormous hot water urns being filled up by a guy in a tank top, shorts, and flip-flops, which she had come to know as the standard uniform for California.

"Can I help?" she asked.

"Nope, this is my commitment and, praise the Lord, it's been keeping me clean for three months now, so you is going to have to find your own job, Lady!"

"Okay," said Deborah, putting up her hands in surrender. She walked out the back door where other members were beginning to gather on the steps and veranda. The sun was setting, and as she walked back to her car she felt a warm feeling, maybe she had found her new home.

The next committee meeting was the following Sunday morning at 8:30 a.m. The 7 a.m. AA meeting was just leaving, and so the chairs were already set up in the Parlor Room. Bob was sitting with another volunteer called Big Joe, so she went in and joined them. Various other women came in, and Bob started the meeting.

"Okay, before old business I want to introduce our newest volunteer, fresh off the boat from across the Pond, Deborah. She trained in London and has worked mostly with PTSD and abuse cases and seems to be an all-around Good Egg." Bob's attempt at an English accent got a few laughs, and everyone welcomed Deborah warmly. Most of the meeting was about funding and policy updates, so it wasn't too exciting, but she got an insight into the people and how the work was divided up. After it was over, the woman sitting next to her put out her hand and introduced herself.

"Hi, I'm Kimberly."

Deborah smiled. "Nice to meet you".

"If you need anything or have any questions, let me know. I have been volunteering here for a few years so please don't hesitate to ask. Bob runs a pretty good show, he is a director after all."

"Really? You mean like a movie director?"

"Well, he did one about 15 years ago. He really wants to be an actor but hey, don't most of the people who come through these doors?"

"Are you an actress?" asked Deborah.

"Oh God no!" answered Kimberly, "I teach special Ed math in an elementary school in Culver City. I just do this to meet guys."

Deborah looked at her.

"Just kidding!" laughed Kimberly. "About the guys I mean. I'm happily married, most of the men who come through here are either weirdos or losers!"

"Got it," replied Deborah, hoping she really was normal.

"So don't be a stranger," offered Kimberly, as they got up and followed the rest of them out the back door.

As Deborah reached the top of the stairs for her first counseling session, she saw a young woman hovering outside the room. She was wearing tight jeans over high-heeled boots, a cute top, and was bright and clean. Her big earrings jangled as she turned to see Deborah approaching. "Hi! Bob said I could come up and wait for you. I'm Kristi."

"Hi, Kristi, nice to meet you. Bob said there was someone here for me to meet. How are you doing?"

"Well, you know," answered Kristi, as they went in.

"Hmm, not really," apologised Deborah, still not quite used to the way Americans talked. "Why don't you tell me." She put her things on the desk, and they both sat in the old, scruffy armchairs in the small room that had a window overlooking the back porch. A palm tree swayed in the ocean breeze as she opened it for some fresh air.

"Okay. So I grew up in Manhattan - New York that is, not Manhattan Beach, blah blah, parents first sent me to the psychiatrist, I guess at about nine. Finished school, nothing to do, got worse, so decided to go to Thailand. My therapist told me I was doing a geographic but whatever and then India and then I thought, hey, why am I running all over the world trying to find myself? I should go back home and be with my own people, right? So I joined a commune on a Native American Indian reservation in Montana, you know, sweat lodges, rain dancing, and all that amazing stuff, but that got really cold in the winter you know so I heard about this retreat place in Malibu and had a break down there, and now I'm here."

"Oh, I see." Deborah didn't really understand any of it. She was not prepared for this. She was confused and wondered what the actual problem was, it sounded like a fantastic life, and clearly, someone else was paying for it all.

"You sound like you were...searching for something?"

"Yes that's right, I'm a searcher, a spiritual searcher. Bob said you were good, only now I'm a wreck and can't even get out of bed unless I have to."

"Why did your parents send you to a psychiatrist when you were nine?"

"Huh? Oh no, everybody went, all my friends went, everyone in my family goes to the shrink."

"But why?" Deborah was so curious. Her very British background was intrigued by this savoir-faire approach to therapy.

Kristi looked confused. Deborah was confused. "I mean, what was the reason, what was it you all needed to talk about?"

"Uhm, life I guess? They told me I had some kinda anxiety disorder. Maybe I was wetting the bed or something. In high school, they told me I was ADD or was it ADHD? And then by the time I went to college, they said I had borderline personality disorder. That's why I had to get out of there, I was sick of all the meds they were giving me. I mean, they gave me one for depression that made me suicidal especially after all the weight it made me put on and so then they give me another one for that! It's ridiculous, now they are medicating me for stuff that they did to me! I couldn't take it anymore. I wanted to try meditation, spiritual stuff instead."

"Good for you. Did you come off all the meds okay?"

"Yes, but it was hard, I had some doctor in India help me. I smoked a lot of weed to get through it, but you know." Kristi paused for a minute. "I just had a thought, quitting Psychiatrists is sometimes harder than getting off the meds! They get their little fingers into your life and won't let you go!"

Deborah smiled and tried not to laugh. "So what was all this anxiety about?"

"Oh you know, life, parents, school, boys, too fat, too thin, teeth not straight enough, grades, too fat again. Life is stressful...life...sucks." Kristi's eyes filled up with tears. She was clearly hurting, but no one, including herself, seemed to know why.

"Life can certainly seem to be very stressful." Deborah struggled for a moment to keep her opinions to herself about how this very privileged spoilt brat had everything and here she was getting subsidized help? "So did any of these spiritual practices help?"

"I like chanting." Kristi sat back in her chair. "It's funny both in India, you know, the mantras and all that, and in the sweat lodges, with the Indians, American Indians. That's funny I guess I like Indians!"

"And so what happened in Malibu?" asked Deborah.

"Ugh, I don't really know. Things were just getting, you know too much. I couldn't sleep at night and couldn't stay awake during the day. I couldn't deal with anyone, and I started crying all the time. I freaked out a few times, you know screaming at everyone for being so mean to me, and they didn't seem to like that. I was told I was disrupting the flow. So I told them where they could stick their flow and I locked myself in my room. They sent for the psychiatrist, and I thought, here we go again, only this time I was thinking what's the point? It's just going to be the same. Things got very dark, and I told Daddy that I didn't want to do that whole Shrink medicated thing again and so I came here. You better fix me, or he's going to have me locked up again!"

"Again?" questioned Deborah, sensing there were some holes in the story.

"Uh, yeah after college they put me in a place for a 'rest' and that's when I said I needed to go to India and then after the sweat lodge incident, they sent me to a retreat place in Tucson, Arizona but if there are bars on the windows and shrinks I don't think that's what most people would call a retreat!"

"Hmm," Deborah was trying to take this all seriously. There was no trauma, as far as she could tell, so what was so wrong?

"So, in all these adventures were you ever...attacked, drugs, drinking? Any... violent outbursts or abuse?" Deborah was searching for hints as to why so much treatment.

"No, not really. Although I have wanted to punch a few people in the face over the years but I never did. The new shrink says I have 'NOS.'"

"NOS?" Deborah felt insecure for a moment, "I haven't heard of that one."

"It's new. My shrink says they just invented it, it's brand new, straight out of the box! He says it's for people just like me."

As soon as Kristi left, Deborah went straight to Bob's office to look up this new mental illness called NOS. Bob was hunched over his desk as usual.

"Do you have a copy of the new DSM 4?" asked Deborah.

"Uh, yes I think it's up on the top shelf, where I keep all the rest of the fiction," answered Bob, sarcastically. "What do you want that for?"

"The girl you sent me, Kristi, says she has NOS, and I felt like an idiot because I didn't know what it was. I thought I should look it up and see what it is before I meet her next time," said Deborah, as she flipped through the gigantic diagnostic manual.

Bob fell back in his chair and grinned. "NOS is it? I might have guessed. It means 'Not Otherwise Specified.' Meaning, if the admitting psychiatrist can't find anything in that massive book to label the patient with, they call it NOS."

"You mean that 'no specific diagnosis' has become a diagnosis?" Deborah was horrified.

"Yep," confirmed Bob. "As soon as I read the reports when the new edition came out I knew it wouldn't be long before it became a label. When we doctors have only twenty minutes to diagnose someone before they can be admitted to a psych unit, NOS is pretty convenient."

"You're a doctor?"

"Yep, Dr. Robert McGowan, psychiatrist, Cornell 1968 if you don't mind."

"But I was told you were trying, I mean, that you are a director?"

"I wanted to be an actor, but of course the parents didn't like that idea, they wanted a doctor. I don't do blood and guts very well, so I did Psych just to get them off my back. Anyway, how do you think we get funding here? A Ph.D. comes in very handy when trying to get your foot in the door of government departments and snotty foundations."

"Are you sure your parents aren't Jewish?" insisted Deborah jokingly.

"Irish Catholic, which is almost as bad when it comes to parental guilt. My brother James is a Bank Manager, and David is a priest, but my sister, Margret, got away with just marrying a doctor," admitted Bob with a grin. "Unfortunately there are more and more young women who are getting this diagnosis when really their problem is that they were born in Beverly Hills!"

"Manhattan," corrected Deborah, raising her eyebrows.

"Same thing."

"She's clearly not stupid, she got into college."

"Don't let that fool you, Daddy probably bought them a new library. God Bless America, you can buy anything you want here. You and I had to work hard for what we have, and in the process, we learned how to deal with life. All these kids who get it given to them on a designer plate just don't know how to cope with life, the poor little darlings. Anyway, she probably got some liberal arts degree."

"What's that?"

"Oh you know, it's one of those Mickey Mouse college degrees where they do some media studies, watch Brad Pitt movies plus two minutes of Psych 101, throw in some Taekwondo and call it an education."

Deborah laughed, she loved Bob's cynical sense of humor, it reminded her of her British friends back home."I sometimes feel like a fraud because I don't have a Ph.D. or some letters after my name."

"Are you kidding me?" scolded Bob. "You have something far more valuable, you have experience. I have met people with PhDs from Stanford to Harvard and put them in a room with a mother whose kid has been killed by a drunk driver, and they don't have a clue. All they know is how to write a prescription, stick a useless label on them, and send the bill. You know what I heard the other day? I was listening to NPR in my car, and I heard this woman being interviewed who had written her Ph.D. thesis on whether pigeons can tell a Picasso from a Monet! This idiot who spent years studying this gets to call herself doctor and you, my dear, get to help people for very little thanks. Now let me know how it goes with Kristi, and if we are lucky, maybe Daddy will buy us a new roof."

12
Pasadena

1995

The phone was ringing as Deborah walked through her front door, she rushed over to pick it up before the caller could hang up.

"Hey, it's Abby, what's up?"

"Not much, just been shopping like you taught me. I spent ages looking for cling film, no one knew what I was talking about. Eventually, I found it only you guys call it Saran Wrap!" laughed Deborah.

"Right, sorry, I forgot to tell you about that one. Anyway, what are you doing this Sunday morning?"

"Hmm...don't know yet, why?"

"Remember I told you about my friend Carol?"

Deborah thought for a moment, "I think so, the yoga teacher, right?"

"Yes, well she and I are going to Pasadena to hear one of our favorite authors speak. He's visiting from Colorado, and I wondered if you wanted to come along? He's amazing, I think you would really like it, and Carol's great to hang out with. We could have brunch after, I know this great place that does eggs benedict you could die for!"

"Uh, ok, thanks! Who's the amazing author?" asked Deborah.

"Oh right. Father Thomas Keating. He's a Trappist Monk but don't be put off by that, his writing is funny and has all kinds of insights, it'll be great!"

promised Abby.

"A funny monk. Ok, then," Deborah wondered what she was letting herself in for.

"We'll pick you up at 9 a.m., byeeee," Abby hung up before Deborah could change her mind.

As they sped inland on the Santa Monica Freeway toward Downtown LA in Abby's new convertible, Deborah couldn't help but see the irony, or was it the comedy of it all. Her, a Jew, with Abby the Southern Baptist, and Carol, a Hare Krishna devotee yoga teacher, all going off to hear a Trappist Monk speak in a Catholic Church! She knew she had arrived in Southern California! The sky was big and clear, and the freeway was almost empty as it was still early on a Sunday morning. They drove through West LA, with the Hollywood sign on their left, and soon the skyscrapers of Downtown came up fast. They merged onto the 101 Freeway to Pasadena with the San Gabriel Mountains in the distance. Beyond, were the snow-capped mountains of Big Bear and Lake Arrowhead. *Glorious*, thought Deborah. She imagined that she would never get used to seeing palm trees and snow all at the same time, and felt a little squeak of excitement to be going somewhere new and unknown.

Abby pulled into the parking lot of a beautiful Californian Monastery. White stucco walls and terracotta tiled roofs were dripping with purple and hot pink bougainvillea. The Mountains rose up just a few blocks away into the fresh morning sky, giving a perfect backdrop to this idyllic scene. They followed the crowd into a courtyard paved with handmade Mexican tiles. Chairs for about 150 people were set up facing a small lectern.

Father Thomas was a tall, thin elderly American. As he walked to the lectern in his monk outfit, Deborah couldn't help thinking he looked like an extra from Star Wars. He wore a long, white robe with a dark brown tabard over the top, which had a hood that although down, stood up high around the back of his head. His hair and beard were shaved very short, and his ears stuck straight out from the sides of his head making him look like a relative of Obi-Wan Kenobi. It was a dramatic contrast to the mostly jeans and T-shirt crowd that had filled the seats. He gave a huge smile and thanked everyone for coming. Deborah was fascinated by his warmth and gentleness. He talked about meditation and something called Centering Prayer, and then told the story of a young man. She guessed immediately that the young man was himself, but it was endearing the way he innocently told it in third person. The young man was a hedonistic pig, apparently, and overindulged in everything while in college. He could drink everyone under the table, got straight As without studying, and was captain of the football team. This was all working fine until one hungover Sunday morning he watched an evangelist preacher testifying on TV. In that moment he knew he should stop his selfish, self-indulgent ways and dedicate his life to God, so he became a monk. Actually, a Trappist monk, who apparently are the severest kind. Hair shirts, bread and water, and by the time it was the end of some long fasting festival, because of his youth and strength he was the only one who wasn't in the infirmary. Ha Ha! He says to himself, I have fasted everyone under the table! The point of the story was that nothing had really changed. Maybe his location, maybe his outfit, but he was still competitive and self-centered. Deborah remembered what Kristi had said about doing a "geographic" to India and how she, herself had moved from Manchester to London in the hope that it would change everything.

Although most of it went over her head, she heard one statement loud and clear:

"We are always looking in the wrong direction for happiness."

It was so simple, so beautiful in its obviousness, that she drank it up. She looked up into the bright, clear morning sky, the Californian sunshine felt so good on her skin.

"Well, what did ya think?" asked Abby, as they sat looking at their menus for brunch.

"Good, really good. I didn't get all the Christian stuff, but he said something that had a deep impact on me."

"Great! Which bit?" Carol couldn't contain her curiosity. "The story about the young man and the geographic? Wherever you go, there you are! You just know he's talking about himself, right?"

"Yes, that was very insightful, but no, I was very struck by the statement, '*We are always looking in the wrong direction for happiness,*'" reflected Deborah.

"Ooh yes, I like that one too. I told you he was good!" agreed Abby.

"In AA we say it's an '*inside job*'" announced Carol.

Deborah was intrigued. "Are you sober?"

"Yes. Hi I'm Carol, and I'm an alcoholic," said Carol playfully. "Why? You sound surprised?"

"No, I mean you seem so..."

"Oops, think carefully before you finish that statement!" interrupted Abby, pulling on Deborah's arm. "She's got 15 years!"

Deborah smiled and tried to think of the right adjective.

"Please don't say *normal*," pleaded Carol, "I'm hardly normal."

"Right, no, um... I think I would say...balanced. You are very balanced. It's a compliment."

"Ok, I've heard worse," admitted Carol with a smile.

"I'm reading a book right now by a woman, I think her name is something Heller, anyway she makes a similar statement, she says, 'The more attached you are to the outside, the less developed you are on the inside and the more developed you are on the inside, the less attached you are to the outside!'" explained Abby.

"Ooh, I like that!" said Carol.

Deborah was soaking this all in. "I've known for a while that it's not the material things that will fix it, but I think he was saying something a little deeper than that."

"It's not that material things don't matter," related Carol, "It's the attachment we have to them that causes all the problems. There is nothing intrinsically wrong with money, security, even fame, but it's what we do to get it and how we react when we don't get what we think we need or deserve, that's the problem.

After the waitress had brought their food, Deborah continued: "But what I think Father Thomas was saying is that when we look outward for the answer, to material things or for people to behave the way we want, we are never going to be truly happy. People and things can't make us happy. It's what we think about them that makes us happy or unhappy. Happiness, real happiness can only come from the inside. Things can't bring us happiness because they put distance between each of us. What we all really want is connection. Happiness is connection."

"I thought my new convertible would make me happy," confessed Abby, "but I still have to get it washed!"

"You poor thing," laughed Carol. "But yes there will never be enough cars or money or fame to give you real, long-lasting happiness. We tell ourselves the lie that it will, but it's always an inside job."

Deborah thought for a moment. "Yes, but it goes deeper than that. Yes, it's a lie that I think the job or relationship can make me happy, but good feelings can only come from inside. I think well-being is always there and true happiness is being ok no matter what is going on on the outside, right? For example, the more you analyse or overthink something, the more you are telling yourself there is something separate from you, something on the outside, that's going to fix it. No wonder anxious thinking makes us...anxious! It confirms the lie that the answer is out there! 'Go for your dreams' is just setting you up for failure because it buys into the lie that something out there is what gives you happiness and connection."

"I agree. I think Father Thomas is saying that if you look inside, the other things, the dreams, will happen. Only not always in the way you thought they would, and when trouble comes you won't be knocked over because it's not real anyway," agreed Carol.

Deborah turned to Carol, "So do you go to the AA meetings at the SMDC? I see they have them there every day?"

"Uh, no. There are thousands of meetings all over town, and the people who go there, well, I doubt if half the room are actually alcoholics."

"What do you mean?" gasped Abby, "Why would anyone go to a yucky AA meeting unless they had to? No offence."

"None taken. You would be surprised. Some are there to get there Court Card signed because they got a DUI, some because their therapist sent them, some because they are looking for love or movie stars, and some because they are lonely and too cheap to pay for group therapy."

"Ok but they could still be alcoholic?" insisted

Deborah.

"Yes, of course. Look, I didn't know what a real alcoholic was before my third sponsor explained it to me, and most people sitting in that place are not!"

"What do you mean, 'real alcoholic'" Deborah was fascinated. "Are there fake ones!?"

"Oh yes!" laughed Carol, clearly enjoying the chance to explain. "I have a friend, Adam, who's been to Treatment 26 times, but he will tell you, all that tells you about him is that he has really good health insurance! According to to the Big Book of Alcoholics Anonymous, there is just one symptom of alcoholism. That is, once you start drinking you can't stop; it's an allergic reaction. That's it, no drama, no hospitals or DUIs needed. And, nowhere in our book does it say that alcoholism, or drug addiction for that matter, is a disease. The Treatment Centers who are making money out of people's misery came up with that. They have watered down the original message so much and sold it back to their patients with their psychobabble nonsense that it won't be long before the AA I got sober in isn't recognisable anymore. Yes, alkies and addicts get into a lot of trouble, but it's not a disease...the problem centers in the mind."

"Making the same mistake over and over expecting a different result," announced Deborah feeling proud she had picked up some of the lingo.

"No!" insisted Carol. "Insanity is making the same mistake over and over *knowing* you are going to get the same result! Either a psychic change has happened, or it hasn't. If the thinking of an alcoholic or addict hasn't changed, eventually they will go back to the booze, the drugs, or the food, or whatever it is for them that kills the pain of being conscious. If their thinking hasn't changed, then nothing will stay changed."

"Ok, on that happy note, coffee anyone?"

announced Abby. "I have to get back to my hubby, he will have finished playing golf by now, and I promised him I would go to Home Depot with him this afternoon."

"Ooh you are so domesticated!" whooped Carol.

"Get lost, you're just jealous."

13
Santa Monica

1995

It wasn't long after her trip to Pasadena with Carol and Abby that Deborah met with a new young client called Lizzie. Bob had suggested that they have a chat, as Lizzie seemed a bit lost and needed some direction. Deborah agreed but she soon got a gut feeling that they weren't going to get very far. They arranged to meet at 9 a.m. after Lizzie's NA breakfast meeting.

"I'm so impressed that you get up so early," complimented Deborah, trying to build some rapport with Lizzie and start the conversation. "I mean, it starts at 7:30 a.m., so you must have to be up at, what 6 or 6:30?"

"Yeah, well I find it helps to get my day going, otherwise I wake up at about lunch time and I don't have much to do to until my shift at the coffee shop at 3."

Lizzie sat back in her chair and folded her arms as if to say, okay let's see what you can do for *me.*

"I see...uh, so where did you grow up?"

"Bakersfield. But I don't like to tell people that, I usually just say Southern California, it sounds better. Bakersfield is so, you know boring, nothing ever happens in stupid Bakersfield," moaned Lizzie, flipping her long, wavy hair back and crossing her legs.

"Okay. So what were you hoping to get out of our chat?" Deborah didn't see any point in delaying the inevitable.

"Well, I need to work on my low self-esteem issues," said Lizzie with an, *isn't it obvious*, almost combative tone in her voice, the irony of which amused Deborah.

"Hmm, and what makes you think you have low self-esteem?" Deborah could hardly hide her amusement.

"What?" snapped Lizzy, surprised.

"I mean, who told you that you have low self-esteem?" asked Deborah, curiously.

"Well, uh, I just do," stated Lizzie, sternly. She was clearly taken aback by this question. "I mean, all my other therapists have told me that I do. I just can't seem to get any of the things I want. All my friends have cute boyfriends or rich husbands or have just come back from the Sundance Film Festival or Hawaii or something."

"So, you're saying you think things like relationships and money will give you self-esteem?" asked Deborah totally fascinated.

"Yeah? Look, I did okay at school, not great, but okay and now I'm working in a coffee shop. It isn't exactly rocket science but I guess mostly relationships are the problem. Guys obviously like to look at me, I mean we all know what guys are like, but they never seem to want to stick around and it's getting me down. They always make me feel so bad about myself and it's ruining my self-esteem."

"And do you think it's your low self-esteem that puts them off, or them leaving that has lowered your self-esteem?" persisted Deborah, trying to get clear on what Lizzie believed.

"What? Both, of course, one leads to the other and it just gets worse and worse. I know I should..." She trailed off into a thought.

"Should what?" prompted Deborah, but Lizzie wouldn't bite. "I see... that's quite a conundrum, I mean you have what seems like an airtight argument there."

"Huh?"

"Well, you said that *they* always make you feel bad, that it's their fault. I would suggest that no one can make anyone feel bad, it just feels like they do."

Lizzie looked confused. "But when someone dumps you, you feel bad and you wouldn't feel bad if they didn't, so clearly it's him that's making me feel bad? My insecurity issues are coming from him," argued Lizzie, getting a little frustrated.

"What's *his* name?" asked Deborah.

Lizzie hesitated, "...Julio."

"Okay. So I know it seems like Julio is responsible for your low self-esteem, but could it be that it's all your thinking about Julio and the relationship that is producing the feelings?"

"What's the difference? He's gone and I feel like...really down?"

"Was he perfect?"

"No, nobody's perfect," responded Lizzie, dismissively.

"Did he ever leave the toilet seat up?"

Lizzy laughed a little. "Yes, sometimes."

"Did he say he was going to be home at a certain time and then not call and leave you waiting for ages?"

"Yes, sometimes. Quite a lot, actually."

"Well, I know this great guy called Marco, he's tall and handsome, about your age. Works in real estate I think. Anyway, he would never leave the toilet seat up, in fact, his mum trained him very well and he always calls if he's going to be late, he's quite the gentleman. Would he make you feel better?"

"Probably," replied Lizzie, half wondering if

Deborah was going to give her Marco's number.

"So it's not Julio that's controlling your self-esteem then, because you just felt better when I told you about Marco. It's the thought that Julio didn't treat you right and the thought that Marco will treat you like a princess that is changing the way you feel about yourself. Marco doesn't even exist, I made him up!"

"That's a shame," snapped Lizzie, angrily flipping her hair again.

"So do you see that your idea that you have low self-esteem because of these outside things is made up? Can I ask you to tell me about a time when you felt you had good self-esteem?"

"Uh... I dunno...when I graduated college, I guess?"

"Okay, great. And what was it about graduating that made you feel good about yourself?"

"I dunno know. I guess I felt good that I had worked hard, that I had achieved something?"

"Right, so it wasn't the actual graduation certificate that the Dean gave you that gave you those good feelings. The good feelings came from inside because you had worked hard and done well. A person can't make you feel bad any more than that piece of paper could make you feel good, it always comes from inside."

"I guess so. But why do they always leave?" pleaded Lizzie, getting frustrated again and changing the subject.

"You said earlier that you did well in school. Can I ask why you are working in a coffee shop?"

"Uh...well... I was going out with this other guy and we were going to get married, we made a lot of plans and then he just left."

"So you decided to look for someone else to take care of you? You know, I think men can tell when we are husband hunting. I mean, can you imagine a guy saying to his buddy, *Wow, I met this really desperate girl last night!*" Lizzie did not find this amusing. "Maybe if you continue to choose jobs that are not fulfilling, hoping that some guy is going to rescue you, you will continue to feel lousy. Maybe it's time to let go of these old ideas?"

Lizzie wasn't interested and changed the subject again. "Well, when I was sharing about my low self-esteem at the meeting this morning, everyone there supported me," she announced defiantly.

Deborah thought for a moment. "I think I saw about eighty, maybe a hundred people leaving that meeting this morning?"

"Yeah... It was pretty full today, why?" asked Lizzie, wondering where this was going.

"Well, I'm not sure how it works in your meetings, but it must have taken a lot of confidence or courage to say yes when they asked you to speak..."

"They didn't ask, I put my hand up to share."

"So you sat in your seat and just started sharing about your very personal feelings in front of all those people?" questioned Deborah, realising she was onto something.

"No, I walked up to the podium and spoke into the microphone."

"Wow! So let me get this straight. You were just sitting in your seat like everyone else and you thought, huh, I need this crowd to listen to me and walked in front of maybe a hundred people and shared about your deepest fears and your *low self-esteem* with no apprehension into a microphone. From a podium??"

"Yes..." mumbled Lizzie, cautiously.

"Lizzie, you don't have low self-esteem, you just think you do!!!!!"

Lizzie stared at Deborah in disbelief.

"Lizzie, do you know what...what confidence it

takes to do what you did this morning? People take classes to be able to do that kind of thing. Acting classes, public speaking classes. And to talk about very personal stuff in front of all those people takes… How can you possibly say you have low self-esteem?"

"But that's what we do in meetings!"

"Some people maybe, the people who can, but plenty of others are sitting in the back terrified, dreaming of being able to do what you did."

Both women sat quietly for what seemed like ages. "I'm wondering, does Julio go to this meeting?"

"Yes."

"Did you want to make him feel bad?"

Lizzie looked down at the floor. She looked out of the window. She looked everywhere except at Deborah. Something was clearly going on in her head so Deborah pushed a little further. "Stunts like that are not going to make him want to come back, Lizzie. Making a man feel bad can never be the foundation of a fulfilling relationship. You are a beautiful, courageous, dynamic young woman who could light up the universe with this kind of passion. Why not direct it to something worthwhile? You could put your passion into so many amazing things that would bring you all the good feelings and security you crave. Now *that* is attractive! There is nothing attractive about appearing desperate or weak, you are meant to be glorious, fabulous, and inspire others to be the same! This idea that you are not good enough when you are on your own, that you need to be with someone or have something to be happy just isn't true. You're perfect just as you are! You have everything you need, you are the perfect expression of what the Universe designed you to be, you have a mission that only you can do and there is no competition for the spotlight in your life other than your old ideas. You are worthy and loveable because you are you! Lizzie, you are looking in the wrong direction for happiness!"

Lizzie looked a little shocked and just stared at Deborah for a few minutes, stunned at what she was hearing. She paused and then reached for her purse, "Thanks for trying to help me but I don't think this is going to work." She got up and walked out the door.

Deborah sat there for a minute knowing that she had messed up. She knew she had pushed too hard too quickly but she couldn't stop herself, from somewhere deep inside it just all came out. Maybe it was what she wanted someone to have said to her back in those dark days in Manchester, or maybe she was angry that this girl who had everything going for her was wasting her life because of some old ideas.

Ugh.

"I messed up!" apologised Deborah walking back into Bob's office.

"Really?" Bob stood up to file some more papers. "I mess up all the time. What happened?"

"I just had a session with Lizzie and I pushed too hard, I preached at her and she left. I'm sorry. I guess I just didn't have any patience for the *poor me* routine today."

Bob laughed. "Well, maybe she heard something, you never know."

"Maybe, but how can these narcissistic, know-it-all, self-assured girls honestly claim to have low self-esteem? ...Chutzpah more like!"

"Well, in Shrink School they would say she is covering up for underlying insecurities," offered Bob, trying to be helpful.

"I get that and I get that they are suffering but most of these girls have concocted some delusional story that the world should treat them a certain way and when it doesn't, they cry victim so they don't have to take any responsibility for their part in it all. I heard someone ask once, who is the most powerful person in a family?" Bob shrugged his shoulders as if to say do tell. "The baby! *Be quiet, the baby is asleep; we have to stop because the baby needs something; don't play that music, the baby doesn't like it* - and on and on. Being the baby, the needy one, gets you a lot of attention and power, so I don't buy this victim crap. She certainly has issues, but low self-esteem, give me a break. It's a label that just gives them permission to get attention, play victim, blame others, and get out of taking any responsibility for their lives!"

"Okay, so when the compassionate Deborah wants to come back, let me know," declared Bob. They both laughed. Bob sat down and invited Deborah to take a seat. "Look, I know it can be hard sometimes, but these kids have often been brought up by the nanny or been tossed from one divorced parent to another, or one or both parents were absent for whatever reason: Could be they were in jail, high on crack, had their heads in a tub of Ben and Jerry's, or out at a board meeting, and they just don't have a clue. Think about it, if you spent all day thinking crappy thoughts, it would have an effect on you right?" Bob sat forward in his chair. "The body is designed in an amazing way. You have heard of fight or flight, right? Well, when that part of the brain, the amygdala, is activated, it sends all kinds of hormones - cortisol, norepinephrine, and glucose - into the body. It's only supposed to be for about twenty minutes, just enough time to get away from the saber-tooth tiger or out of the burning house. But if you sit there and worry for two hours, eight hours, sixteen hours, all day, day after day, it's going to mess with your body chemistry. Most of the people who come in here have often done the rounds of school psychologists, therapists, and social workers and not found any answers. At least they haven't given up, they are still searching for something. We can only hope."

Deborah sighed. "I know. Okay, I'll let you know when compassionate Deborah gets back but she might want a pay raise!"

The next day Deborah was out for a stroll with her neighbour Sheldon. They had heard that 60s guitar legend Dick Dale was playing an impromptu gig in the skateboard park at the beach in the middle of the afternoon, so they had gone over to enjoy the free entertainment. Once the spectacle was over they sat for a while watching the tourists go by. Venice Beach was a big tourist spot with its boardwalk of coffee shops, T-shirt stands, tattoo parlours, and the famous Muscle Beach Gym where guys worked out in the open for everyone to see. Sheldon was a counsellor at the V.A. He'd been in Vietnam and as an ex-patient, he would go there to volunteer. He was gentle and kind and an engineer at the Pasadena Jet Propulsion Lab, and one of the few people she knew who wasn't in the film business.

"I had this curious encounter with a young woman yesterday. She was convinced she had low self-esteem but she was one of the most confident, self-assured people I have ever met! She actually said that men *obviously* like to look at her, I had the hardest time not laughing, no low self-esteem there! And she has no problem speaking in front of a hundred people about her feelings at the drop of a hat. I'm not sure I could do that!"

Sheldon laughed, "Yikes!"

"There seems to be a sense of entitlement that makes certain people shocked when the world doesn't treat them right. It's as if they have shown up here in LA expecting we are all going to fall at their feet and take care of them. It's almost like they have too much esteem!" accused Deborah.

"I know what you mean. Many people look around at what others have worked hard for and they think they should have it too just because they showed up," agreed Sheldon.

"Right, a person with low self-esteem would believe that they aren't good enough to deserve any of it. They wouldn't expect the world to fall at their feet. They would be shocked and surprised, not hurt and resentful."

"I agree, I see it all the time," continued Sheldon, finishing his ice cream.

"Yes! To expect someone to treat me great and that everything should always go my way are thoughts that are coming from an ego out of control, an ego that is up there somewhere sitting on a throne demanding what it wants. That's not low self-esteem! That's out of control, self-obsessed, narcissistic, conceited, what-about-me, ME ME ME esteem! And when it doesn't go their way, they say it's our fault!" cried Deborah, laughing at her own realization.

"Ha, you just reminded me of what I saw in the market yesterday," laughed Sheldon. "This guy was standing in the ten-items-or-less line at the checkout and he was going off on the woman in front of him because she had fifteen things. It was hilarious, he was going, *How dare you? You are making me late, you're killing me!*" He was having a meltdown, the poor guy. He was convinced that this woman was the cause of his discomfort. Problem is when we're in that painful place it's very hard to see that it's your thinking and not the stupid person in front of you."

14
Malibu

Carol had called and asked Deborah if she wanted to go for a walk along the beach in Malibu, it sounded like a nice treat, so they made a plan to meet in about an hour. She picked Deborah up, and they drove for about twenty minutes up the Pacific Coast Highway to Malibu Pier. On their left were some surfers out in the clear, turquoise Pacific Ocean, hoping to catch a wave before work, and to the right, the rugged Malibu cliffs rose high, straight up from the side of the road. They found a parking spot alongside the highway and Deborah treated them both to ice cream. It was a bright, clear morning, and the two women took off their shoes to walk along the beach through the small breaking waves, picking up shells and enjoying the warm spring sunshine.

"You're not teaching yoga today?"

"I already gave a class early this morning. I just thought it would be nice to get out. Sometimes I forget the beach is here, so I make a point of coming when I think about it."

"Ha," laughed Deborah, "I haven't been here long enough to forget about it, I still have to pinch myself sometimes that I'm so lucky to live a few minutes' walk from the sand."

Carol picked up an interesting looking piece of driftwood that had been caressed by the ocean, just as a large wave caused the two women to jump with surprise. They ran back up the beach to escape, then sat on the sand for a while to dry off.

"I had a new client this week and I messed up big time," Deborah was still preoccupied with her conversation with Lizzie. She lay back on the white sand to relax. "She got on my nerves, and I started to preach at her."

"Ooops."

"Yeah, big Ooops. It didn't feel good, but I started to see how much we actually create our own reality. Bob was telling me about how our bodies produce all these chemicals and stress hormones that are only meant to be in our system for a short time, you know fight or flight, but apparently, if you spend hours and hours a day worrying, then the body will overload with...cortisol, glucose, and adrenaline, and actually change your body or something. I can't remember all the science, but it made me think about how many people are sitting in misery and ignorance because they don't understand what they are doing to themselves just by worrying all day!"

Carol looked at her incredulously.

Deborah sat up. "It's fascinating, I went and looked it up. You must have heard those stories about how a wife can lift a car off her husband after an accident or a man swims through shark-infested water to save his kid? Well, it's because the brain puts all these survival chemicals into the body and shuts down the parts of the body you don't need in an emergency, like the digestive system and the immune system. I mean, it all makes sense: if you spend hours a day in anxiety and fear, just think of all those stress chemicals that are flooding your system, and they don't get a chance to leave before more are pumped in. The bit that scares me is that it shuts down parts of the brain!

"Like what?" Carol looked around alarmed.

"Well, I guess in an emergency, you don't need to be able to be creative or available to new ideas or plan things for the future; when you are running out of a burning building, you just need to get out. Apparently, all these teenagers who sit in stress all day are getting early-onset diabetes because of all the extra glucose that is going into their bodies!"

"Yikes," exclaimed Carol, "that's frightening! No wonder depressed people can't see anything positive ahead."

"Exactly! I didn't understand any of this when I was sitting in Manchester reliving and reliving my attack day after day. No wonder I felt so bad physically! I was exhausted, and I just couldn't think straight. It was like I was in a thick fog, and it just made doing anything a hundred times harder."

"Wow," Carol was having a hard time taking this all in. "Just imagine, there must be thousands of people sitting in mental hospitals who have made *themselves* sick?!"

"I know! And these medications that are supposed to help cause so many more problems. Did you know your intestines have serotonin receptors?"

"What!?" cried Carol. "I thought serotonin was in the brain?"

"It is but there are receptors in other parts of the body as well, now you know why people on antidepressants get stomach problems. And get this, apparently, it was just a marketing technique to say that there is a chemical imbalance in the brain, that antidepressants are like insulin for diabetics. It was just an analogy to help sell the drugs and the drug company doctors never corrected it! They stuck with the story that it did something to balance the brain, which was caused by overthinking in the first place and then get you addicted! Brilliant marketing!

Apparently, your immune system has serotonin receptors too, so no wonder depressed people keep getting sick all the time, it's a vicious cycle!"

"That's a scary thought," reflected Carol, "and you know those doctors are getting massive kickbacks from the pharmaceutical companies!"

"They are making millions out of people misery, most of which they created themselves! I'm so glad I didn't get caught up in that kind of a mess, some people never get out."

They sat for a while longer soaking up the morning sun, then slowly made their way back up the beach, splashing in the water.

"I just realised something..." pondered Deborah. "If it's not happening right now, it's not real."

15
Universal Studios

1996

Being self-employed was always good practice for seeing how well Deborah was doing with the quality of her thoughts. She thought about what Father Thomas had said about looking in the wrong direction for happiness and felt a beautiful calmness come over her. Thinking about when or if the next job was coming made her feel stressed, but realising that nothing in the room had changed, just her thoughts about her life, made her feel calm. *Look at that*, she thought, *my thoughts are governing how I feel.* When she thought about her bank balance for a moment and how long the money from the last movie would last, she could feel her blood pressure go up, or whatever it was that made you have that icky feeling in the pit of your stomach. She stopped and thought about how lucky she was to be in California, with a beautiful home in the Venice Canals and the luxury of time to enjoy it all. She had learned from Shelly that her thoughts were the problem, and she had worked hard at replacing them with positive ones, but this was different. She watched a family of ducks swim by in the canal in front of her house and then decided to go visit Sheldon and his wife Jennifer for a cup of tea and a chat, then on Monday she would make some calls about work.

Deborah was looking forward to her next meeting with Kristi, and now that she knew what N.O.S. was, she felt confident that she could help, but Kristi didn't show. She read one of Father Thomas's books while she waited until Dee, another volunteer, put her head around the door.

"Kristi just called to say she is sorry but she just can't make it today, life is, you know too much for her right now or something like that."

"Thanks," Deborah was disappointed. "Dee, do you have a minute? Can I ask you a question?"

"Sure, I have a few before my compulsive shoplifter shows up," replied Dee as she stood in the doorway.

"You are a psychiatrist right?"

"Analytical psychologist actually. I work in a clinic, and I have a private practice in Brentwood. I come here a couple of times a week partly to do Bob a favour, but mostly because it looked good on my resume, I'm retiring soon. I've been a practicing psychologist for over 40 years, but I'm not a saint like you and Bob." Dee looked at her over her reading glasses as the gold chain that dangled from the sides caught the light. Her short hair had been dyed red in an attempt to give her a jaunty air, but she still seemed very business-like and didn't quite fit in with this very casual, laid back place.

"Okay, not sure about that, I sometimes come because I'm bored," reflected Deborah honestly. "Anyway it's like this, is it possible that if you ignored your thoughts, they would just go away? I mean, can thoughts die of neglect?"

Dee looked at her sideways. "Yes, but don't tell anyone or I'll be out of a job!" she left, and Deborah listened to her footsteps as they faded down the wooden stairs.

Deborah laughed to herself, she had suspected it for a long time, she just felt like she needed a professional to confirm it... She went back to her book.

A few days later Deborah sat at home secretly watching Oprah when the phone rang.

"Hi, this is the Director of Operations at Universal Studios, I was given your number by Stan Winston."

Deborah was taken aback. Who? What? And why had Stan Winston given them her number? Stan Winston was a multi-Oscar-winning visual effects giant, and she had never actually worked with him, and it was a few years since his colleague Michael Lantieri had watched her fix that dinosaur nose... "Who is this?"

"We are about to open 'Jurassic Park: The Ride' in two days, and we are behind schedule; how soon can you get here?"

Deborah thought it must be a joke, but he kept going. "We need your help on the dinosaurs, and Stan said you supervised on *The Flintstones*?"

"Yes I did, but I'm in Venice Beach, it would take me an hour at least to get there?" estimated Deborah, still not sure what was happening.

"Great! I will put your name on the gate, just come straight to the ride."

Deborah put down the phone and paused for a moment. What just happened? Oh well, she thought to herself, either this is a joke or not, but a story either way. She grabbed her toolkit and drove to Universal Studios, not knowing what to expect.

Almost to her surprise, her name was on a list at the gate of the Back Lot, and the security guard directed her to where she should park. Deborah made her way to the ride and was immediately set to work. "At the beginning of the ride, the guests sit in boats and gently flow along an underwater track through everglades as brontosauruses stick their heads high up out of the water as if eating and browsing, all very nice. Problem is, whoever sculpted their heads did so with their mouths closed and now they are being moved by the mechanics put inside, their faces are ripping apart!" said a frantic project supervisor.

"They should have been sculpted half-open, latex can only stretch so much," said Deborah confidently.

"I know! If I get my hands on the amateur who...anyway, can you fix them?"

Deborah looked over at the dinosaurs, they were sticking at least 15 feet up in the air above the waterline. "How deep is that water?" she asked nervously.

"Only about 4 feet."

"Well, I know I'm tall, but I'm not that tall. How am I supposed to get up there?" Deborah covered her eyes from the hot sun and pointed up to their heads.

"Oh, we have a ladder, that's not a problem, just climb off one of the boats," instructed the supervisor and left.

Before she knew it, Deborah was up a 20-foot ladder that was 4 feet in water under the blazing California sun giving a brontosaurus a facelift. Other workers, mostly men, were all around fixing lights and cables, arranging plants and trees, as the movie soundtrack played over and over in the background. After a few hours, she was done, very hot, and sick to the back teeth of the theme to *Jurassic Park*.

After a short break, Deborah was assigned another job inside. More dinosaur facelifts, only this time as a car repeatedly fell over a rock inches from her head, and another where the whole wall cracked open like a never-ending earthquake. She and the large team of artists and maintenance men worked late into the night and then were asked back the next day. Early the next morning, she arrived at the site to be told that the main T-Rex needed fixing. "For the finale of the ride, the boats dive over this waterfall and as you drop, a massive angry T-Rex comes through the waterfall and just misses taking a bite out of you as you drop down there. Cool right?" explained the supervisor pointing down an 85-foot drop of rushing water.

"Uh, sure but I don't think anyone has a ladder that tall," Deborah took a nervous step backwards.

"No problem, we have climbing gear for you. You can be lowered down and then work right on his nose, see there where it's ripped?"

"What!"

Deborah was handed a hard hat and a climbing harness, and two very keen props guys helped her in and onto a hoist. She was then lowered down as 1000s of gallons of water rushed past her at great speed, the noise of which almost drowned out the never-ending Jurassic Park theme music. At least it was cool inside, but wow, she was now 85 ft in the air above a deep pool of foaming water. She looked around, how did she get here?! Suddenly it occurred to her that she had not signed any paperwork or agreed on a fee! This, she decided, was the last assignment for her and she pictured herself safe and dry at home watching Oprah again by 3 p.m.

16
Beverly Hills

1996

Deborah was hopefully meeting Kristi today. She was curious about what had happened to make her miss her last session and a little worried that her family had taken her off to some prison-type Treatment Center again, but thank God she was safe and showed up as planned.

"So what happened the last few weeks? I was looking forward to seeing you again!" asked Deborah gently.

"I dunno, it all got too much. I really liked talking to you but my parents want to see results, you know, they just don't trust me to get it together."

"That must feel like a lot of pressure?"

"Yes, that's exactly it. Pressure. All this, it feels like so much pressure and I can't cope with it," cried Kristi, pointing to her head.

"I have an idea," offered Deborah. "Maybe the pressure that you are feeling is coming from your own thoughts, from the story you keep telling yourself?"

"Of course it is! I think about how my parents want me to do better, I think about how my ex-boyfriend wanted me to be skinnier, I think about how all my friends have amazing jobs. If all these people would just leave me alone and let me..." Kristi trailed off.

"Well yes, I was thinking maybe it's not the events

or the parents that cause the pressure, but it's actually the thoughts about the parents and the others that are making you feel this uncomfortable?"

"You haven't met my parents! By the way, they are here staying with my aunt and uncle in Beverly Hills, so we better be on our best behavior," said Kristi waving her finger at Deborah jokingly.

"Stay with me a moment. Your mind wants you to focus on what they are all doing wrong, but really it's your thoughts about what they are all doing that is causing you this distress; could you see that?" Deborah paused to see if Kristi would get it.

"You mean, if I didn't think about them, I wouldn't feel bad? Of course I get that, that's why I like pot and that's why they want to fill me with meds so I won't think or feel!"

"No, I'm not talking about blocking it out with pills or smoking something. I'm talking about recognizing it for what it is, just thoughts, just…I dunno know, just stuff, energy I guess, that moves through your head. Your parents are not here right now in this room, just your thoughts about them."

Kristi looked up. She jokingly looked around the room and then picked up a cushion as if to check if her parents were there. "Maybe they are hiding behind that plant, they are pretty sneaky," alleged Kristi sarcastically. "No, but you can't just tell yourself to shut up? That's nuts"

"I did," admitted Deborah, cautiously.

"Did it work?"

"Yes, but it was brutal. And it was before I understood how my mind actually worked. You see, what I have come to understand is that if you ignore your thoughts, the ones that are making you feel bad, the ones that say *should* or *I messed up* and *oh crap I messed up again,* you can put them over there in the corner and ignore them. They will go away if you just ignore them."

"Mine don't. You don't understand what it's like in here," confessed Kristi, pointing to her head again. "This committee is out to get me!"

"I know it can feel like that, but that's the point. Your feelings are coming from your thinking. Think about this for a moment: You know how if you stay in the bath or the swimming pool for too long, your skin starts to wrinkle?"

"Yeah, I hate that," agreed Kristi.

"But it doesn't if you are only in there for a short while, right? Well, that's what happens with our minds. If we stay too long in the negative thoughts, our minds get all contaminated and wrinkly, and if you spend hours a day in negativity, it will lead to panic attacks and depression. At least that's what happened to me."

"Huh," mumbled Kristi. "No wonder my mother looks terrible; she's all wrinkled up like a prune from all that worrying!"

"See if this helps? Imagine you are sitting in the cinema waiting for the movie to start, and the couple in front of you are speaking in Russian or Farsi or some language you don't understand."

"I understand Farsi, my family on my father's side are Persian."

"Okay then, Russian. Imagine the couple in front of you are speaking Russian, but because you don't understand Russian, you just ignore it, you don't get sucked in."

"Ha, that's funny. When I was a kid, my grandparents would talk about my mother in front of her in Farsi, but she couldn't understand. She's from Long Island, so she never knew what they were saying about her."

"Exactly. So in that moment, she was not affected by what they were saying. If you don't get sucked into the negative conversation in your head, you won't *feel* negative, it's that simple."

Kristi thought for a moment. "Okay but...what if someone deliberately hurts you or a big dog is going to attack you? You can't ignore those thoughts."

"Of course not, it's normal to be hurt if someone you know or love hurts you, and it would be normal to be scared if a big dog comes at you with its big teeth. But that's in the moment. Most of the anxious thinking that hurts us is either after the fact, by going over and over what happened, or thinking about the future, worrying and worrying about what might happen. But it's not happening right now. You'd have to ask yourself why you are deliberately making yourself feel bad now."

"I never considered that I was doing it to myself before," wondered Kristi. "That's kind of weird?"

"But it's also good news. If you are the one doing the negative thinking, then you can stop it. It might be hard at first, it might have become a habit, but it is possible."

"So, if what you are saying is replace it with positive thoughts, I've tried that. All those therapists and gurus would suggest that. *Imagine your mother as a pure soul, send out good vibes and you will get good vibes back*, blah blah blah. But it never worked because I would find myself in the middle of one of those pity parties, realize I've done it again, and then beat myself up for not remembering to be positive!"

Deborah agreed that that was not the answer, she knew there must be something else. "I think positive thinking is better than negative thinking, but really it's just more thinking, right? Maybe we need to smash this whole thinking-control project on the head?" Deborah stopped for a moment as a picture came into her mind. "You know those bubbles that kids blow, the ones made of soapy water?" Kristi nodded. "Well, when you try to catch them they...poof! Just disappear, right? Well, most of our thoughts are like that. They just blow past us, we don't even register them, and if we even see them they just...poof into thin air when they land on us, right? Now, imagine I threw ping pong balls at you. It would be annoying as they bounced off, but they wouldn't hurt. There are some thoughts that are like that - *ugh I need to pay the rent, he's such an idiot, when is the traffic going to move* - annoying, but they pass, too. And then there are thoughts that hit you like a...like a basketball and almost knock you out. They shock you so much that you replay and replay it over and over."

"Yes! I got hit on the head with a basketball once at school and I swear I saw stars! It stayed with me for days!" exclaimed Kristi.

"Well, you and I understand how different balls work. If we understood how thoughts work, we wouldn't be scared of them, we would know that it's just a bubble, it's just a ping pong ball, or ouch! That was a basketball!! But what if you could see the basketball coming? You could maybe dodge it and it would just pass on by like all the others?"

"I don't know," Kristi thought for a moment. "Sounds a bit too simple, it's not that easy. There was no way I could have seen that basketball coming, and it really hurt."

"Okay, but after it hit you, you had a choice: you could see it was an accident and let it go, or you could think about it over and over and make it worse. And what if you stopped and asked yourself, What are these basketballs here to tell me?" offered Deborah getting mixed up with her metaphors. "Let's talk about it more next time, but I think we are onto something here!"

Deborah's schedule at the SMDC started to fill up, and over the course of the next year, she got into a nice routine of seeing clients, making new friends, exploring LA, and working. She added two more big movies to her resume, and in between filming, she started going to Carol's yoga classes and even tried some meditation classes with Abby. It was all very Californian, but she started to notice that instead of the war zone her inner life had been, it was now a tranquil neighborhood, free from all that chaos and fear, and if any scary or negative thoughts came, she would just get the thought police in to shoo them away.

After a few more sessions, Kristi came bouncing into the counselling room to see Deborah.

"Wow, you look like you're in a good mood?" observed Deborah.

"I don't know what you have been doing to me, but I haven't smoked pot in a whole week!"

"Uh, well that's good, were you smoking a lot before?" Deborah suddenly felt a bit naive.

"Pretty much every day; it dulled the pain in my head."

"And now there's no pain?" asked Deborah hopefully.

"Well, I wouldn't say there's *no* pain, the world's an ugly place at times if you watch the news, but I kept picturing bubbles and ping pong balls coming at me like you said. But where did the pain go? I'm not complaining, but what did you do to me?" accused Kristi flopping into the chair with a big smile.

"You *sure* you haven't been smoking something?" inquired Deborah as they both laughed.

"No, but this really cool thing happened! I had to go for dinner with my parents and the rest of them, you know *the family*, and my mother said some really annoying stuff like she always does, and I started to get all messed up like I always do. You know, my head started, like, *she is always criticizing me, nothing I do is right, they want me to be miserable*, and I started feeling down, anxious, like I wanted to run or smoke. Then suddenly, I became very aware of my thoughts, like I could actually hear them, kind of like I was overhearing them or something, and I thought to myself, hmmm, so what are these thoughts about? And I suddenly realized they weren't even true! My parents don't want me to suffer, in fact, they have done everything they can so that I won't suffer. The thoughts were all lies, it's my stupid thoughts that have made me feel so anxious that I have to run. And then - you won't believe it - poof! Just like that, the thoughts stopped. Just like that, they went away like those kids' bubbles! I didn't even have to picture my mom as a pure soul or some stupid thing. Before I knew it I was chatting away with my grandmother and playing with my nephews. I was having a good time, *with my family*!"

"Wow!" cried Deborah, amazed that it was happening so quickly. She had presumed it would take years to change that kind of thinking. She wondered for a moment why people needed to be in therapy for so long if change like this was possible after a few months.

"You don't understand, I haven't had a good time, even an okay time with my family since I was about eight years old! The twisted thing was, I almost wanted to have a fight with my mother just to see if I could do it again!"

"Wow," repeated Deborah. "You are a miracle of mental health!"

They both laughed and Deborah listened as Kristi talked about her new experiences. It was so great to see her comfortable with herself.

"They are here for a few more days and then they want me to go with them to Hawaii, but I'm not sure about that. Maybe too much for me just yet?"

"I think you have to trust yourself, you know what you are able to cope with."

"Right. I think I will wait. My sister is getting married in the spring so maybe that would be a good time to try it again?" decided Kristi, answering her own question.

"That sounds wonderful. And what about you? What do you want to do?"

"How do you mean?" Kristi looked confused.

"Well, you went to college, you got some kind of degree, right?"

"Yeah, I have a Masters in International Communications, what about it?"

"Uh...yeah, exactly," Deborah was thrown for a second. "What about doing something with that?"

"Never thought about it. It just seemed something cool to study to keep my parents off my back."

"Okay, so why not think about it now? Now that your mind isn't all busy with the anxiety and worrying, you could maybe think about a job? International Communications sounds pretty cool!"

"I guess, it would be nice to be independent of the parents."

"Okay, so let's see what comes."

A few weeks later, Kristi came with some news.

"I got a job!" she announced like a proud kid who had just learned to tie her shoes.

"Amazing!" Deborah was thrilled and fascinated to hear what had shown up.

"My landlady is a doctor, some kind of specialist surgeon at UCLA, and she was telling me that she needed someone to help her organize her stuff, you know, appointments and papers, that kind of stuff. So I said I can do that for her and hey, she's paying me to come twice a week to organize her life! I might as well put that OCD diagnosis to some use!"

"That's fantastic! Like a personal assistant?"

"Yeah, I guess so. Her kids are all grown up and her husband died recently and she invented some heart stent thing, so she is brilliant and really busy."

"I'm so happy for you; doesn't it feel good to be contributing and helping someone. She sounds amazing."

"Yeah, she is. I think it helps to be thinking about something or someone else for a change. I'm beginning to see how much of my day I was thinking about myself. No wonder my self-esteem was always in the toilet, I just kept thinking how bad I was, all day long!"

"But, did you? Did you really think you were bad or that your parents were bad for not treating you right?" asked Deborah.

"What's the difference?"

"Well, I have heard a lot of people talk about their low self-esteem since I've been here in California, and when I ask them about it, it usually comes down to a belief that other people aren't treating them right. But surely, if I had low self-esteem and you treat me badly, then that would make sense to me, right? I mean, if I really believed I'm not worth anything and you treat me like dirt, then that would make sense, no?" Kristi listened intently. "But if you treat me badly and I'm upset, then surely I must think that you should treat me better because I believe I should be treated better, do you see?"

"I guess so?" Kristi paused for a moment. "Actually, I always thought I was just a spoiled brat, but all those therapists kept telling me I had low self-esteem and that sounded much better!" admitted Kristi laughing. "I mean, it feels better to say I have a diagnosis then to tell someone I'm just spoiled!" They both fell about laughing.

"Exactly!" agreed Deborah. "It's so much easier to blame other people for our low feelings, but that's exactly it. We create our own little worlds, and when people or situations don't live up to our expectations, we blame others for our low feelings. It's like someone who prays for rain, then goes outside and complains it's raining!! We create our own little Hells and then want to blame someone else! *It can't be my fault!*"

Kristi continued to see Deborah and she continued to have insights into her own story. Sometimes Deborah wasn't sure who was helping who at times and cherished their time together. As the months went by, she felt like she had a front row seat in the unfolding of *Kristi: The Miracle.* She loved to see how the universe was unfolding for her the same way it had for herself once she got out of her own way. Kristi's boss, Dr. Saunders, was in big demand, and soon she needed Kristi more and more. First, she took her to New York for a medical conference on heart surgery and then to Sacramento for some legislative work. It was almost a year to the day since they had first met when she got some more great news.

"She's just finished writing a book about how to keep your heart healthy, so we are going on a book tour for a few months!" announced Kristi. "We might even be going to Europe!"

"So look, your Masters in International Communications is coming in useful after all!"

"Yes! My parents are really pleased. Which reminds me, it's my sister's wedding next week, a whole week of the family... Do you think I'm ready?"

"I think you can do anything you want to! It was only your thinking that was holding you back, it was telling you lies and you chose to believe them and now that you understand how your mind works, you can ignore them. That's real freedom."

"But the funny thing is," admitted Kristi, "they just don't come anymore. Well, sometimes, but they seem to have died of neglect like you said they would. I was telling Dr. Saunders's daughter all about it. She's a psychiatrist. She wasn't convinced, but when I told her about all the labels and diagnoses and meds I used to be on, she was amazed."

Deborah smiled. "You are amazing."

17
Marina Del Rey

1996

Deborah had several regular clients by now, but there was always someone who only needed one or two appointments. This week, Bob had asked if she could fill in for Dr. Dee, as she needed to be out of town for a few days. Apparently, it was imperative for this young man to have his weekly session and Deborah had agreed, so she read up a little in his file. The young man was a Gulf War Veteran, he had a whole alphabet of diagnoses and labels, from PTSD, borderline personality disorder, suicidal ideation, and something called Gulf War Syndrome. It was the first time she would work with a male client and she was looking forward to the opportunity.

Anton was about 28 and struck Deborah as very sad as he walked in and slumped into the chair opposite her. She asked a few general questions just to break the ice, so they chatted for a while about music and surfing, and then Anton said: "Aren't you going to ask me about what happened?"

"Only if you want me to?" offered Deborah.

Anton shrugged his shoulders. "But that's what Dee does and all the other therapists and Psychiatrists they send me to at the V.A.?"

"Has it helped?" inquired Deborah.

"No, not really, it just makes me miserable to keep having to talk about it over and over. I come in feeling okay, and then they ask me to go back and remember all that terrifying stuff, my mum dying, our Unit getting ambushed, and all that death. Some of them want me to write about it and read it out again and again and tell them what I feel about it, and I leave feeling like, well crap. Excuse me, ma'am!"

Deborah looked at him and all of a sudden, she couldn't help herself, she burst out laughing! Anton looked a little shocked, and then he started to laugh too, and before they knew it, they were both laughing their heads off.

"I'm so sorry!" apologised Deborah feeling totally irresponsible. "That wasn't very professional of me, but it sounded so silly when you say it like that. You go to them to feel better, and you leave feeling worse! I know it's not funny at all but..." and she started to laugh again. "I'm so sorry!"

"No, you're right," exclaimed Anton. "It's hilarious when you put it that way. I don't understand it, but that's what they say will help. Dr. Dee calls it Flooding Therapy, and now they are trying something new called Emotional Reprocessing Therapy or something and that I should expect to feel worse first! I wonder sometimes who is the crazy person, me or them?!"

They calmed down and sat quietly for a few minutes.

"Anton, what do you think it would take for you to feel better, to have peace of mind?"

Anton thought for a moment, he looked confused. "I...I'm not sure, they have always told me that I'm damaged goods, that I need to keep looking at my past to find out what my triggers are and all that junk. Are you saying I don't have to?"

"I don't know," admitted Deborah, "I just think you could have some peace if you wanted."

"Of course I want peace, to be happy, but...it's like

someone is holding my happiness out there in front of me and I can't quite reach it. I struggle with flashbacks and nightmares, I wake up screaming sometimes. I don't really have friends, and I just feel weighed down by it all. I just have too much baggage."

A thought went through Deborah's mind - she could almost see it go from one side of the room to the other - *Emotional baggage is made of thought, it's just thought.*

"Hmmm," Deborah paused. "I thought I did too, and when I was asked if I was ready to let go of it, it felt very threatening. I had my skull fractured in a nightclub, then I was attacked and beaten up by three guys, and then my neck was broken another time by a teenage mugger. I'm sure it's nothing like what you have been through, but I got very sick after, very dark depression, couldn't sleep or eat and started hurting myself. The Shrink said I needed to keep talking it out, but going over it again and again never made sense to me either, so I stopped going." Deborah paused again and looked him straight in the eye. "Anton, I'm here to tell you that I got well, I got free of it all without digging around in the past, and so can you!"

Deborah walked into the SMDC office a few days later. "I got your message, Bob, what did you want to see me about?"

"Uh, yes. Well, it's kind of...difficult but, hmm...well, see Dee has a problem...with you, and she wants us to all have a chat, sorry."

"What?!" exclaimed Deborah, nervously. "What did I do?!"

"Well, you're the new girl, and you have rocked a very old and steady boat. Dee has been here a long time and feels... Anyway, she can tell you."

Right on cue, Dee came in and sat down. "So glad

we could have this little chat, my dear." Deborah felt immediately patronized, and a little ganged up on. "So, last week when I was out of town, you very kindly took one of my clients for me?"

"Yes," acknowledged Deborah, wondering what was coming next.

"Yes, well Anton has decided he wants to continue his work with you and stop working with me after two years of intensive critical analysis. We are at a crucial stage in his treatment, and now you have just waltzed in and ruined everything!"

Deborah was shocked and quite taken aback.

"I know you are not professionally trained, so it seems I am going to have to tell you that it is not okay to interfere in someone else's treatment plan or steal someone else's client!"

Deborah was speechless.

"Now, Dee, as I asked before," insisted Bob, trying to keep things calm, "Did Anton actually tell you that Deborah encouraged him to change?"

"No, but she obviously hinted to him that he would be better off working with her!"

"Wow, that is just not true!" replied Deborah in total disbelief.

"Well, I don't know how they do it in London, but here we respect boundaries and professional relationships," accused Dee, folding her arms in disgust.

"Okay, what exactly did Anton say that I said?"

"Well, he left a message saying thank you very much and that he will be working with you from now on."

"But you must have talked to him, what were his reasons?"

"I haven't actually spoken to him yet, I wanted to hear from you first," demanded Dee, indignantly.

"Hold on," interrupted Bob, trying to calm things

down. "So you haven't even heard why or what actually happened? How can you accuse Deborah of anything?"

"I might have guessed you'd be on the side of the cute, young girl!"

"I am not a *girl*!" insisted Deborah sternly and stood up.

"Sorry, young woman then, but you must have said something that led him to that decision?"

"I hardly said anything, I just listened. He told me he was tired of going over and over the past and I asked him what did he think it would take for him have peace of mind, that's pretty much it."

"Why on earth would you ask him that?" asked Dee, incredulously. "He doesn't have any idea what he wants or what it would take!"

"Have you ever asked him?" demanded Deborah.

"Of course not, that would be like asking a kid if they want candy! He's just going to say he wants to have peace of mind!" argued Dee raising her voice.

"And what would be so wrong with that! Don't we all deserve to have peace of mind? Why is Anton not allowed the same chance for peace and happiness like the rest of us?"

"Yes, very nice speech my dear, but he has so many issues, you have no idea what he's been through, he can't just decide to be happy, you are being ridiculous!!" shouted Dee.

"Okay, you have called me unprofessional, a girl, and now ridiculous. I think we are done here," concluded Deborah, heading for the door.

"Uh, Debs, don't go!" pleaded Bob helplessly, but it was no good, Deborah had had enough.

As soon as she got home, there was a message on her answer machine. It was Bob asking her to call.

"Debs, I am so sorry," apologised Bob.

"How could you let her ambush me like that?"

"I didn't know she was that angry!"

"You're scared of her!" accused Deborah patronizingly.

"Me? Uh, well...maybe a little," admitted Bob. But she has been here so long, longer than me, and she has all these credentials that look good for the Center, and she does help a lot of people."

"I'm sure she does, but I guess Anton was ready for something new. I really didn't encourage or hint at anything. Has no one spoken to him about this yet?"

"No, he just left that message that I should change his appointments to you."

"Okay, just get this sorted, Bob, but I'm not the bad guy here!"

Kimberly had asked Deborah over for coffee several times, and now seemed a good time to get together. She lived with her husband and young son in a modern apartment overlooking the beach in Marina del Rey, just a few blocks south of the Venice Pier. They sat on the balcony with the fresh sea air blowing in from the Pacific Ocean. Across the wide stretch of white beach, Deborah could just see the ocean, a far-off gorgeous strip of turquoise joining it to the clear, blue sky.

"I love living here. The tourists don't come down this far, so it's nice and quiet." Kimberly put down two cups of herbal tea on the table and invited Deborah to join her.

"This is a long way from my flat in London," reflected Deborah, "but you know what, I still sometimes miss the grey skies, the rain, and the rumble of the underground train going by."

Kimberly looked at her to see if she was being

sarcastic. "Are you being sarcastic? I can never tell with you Brits."

"Just a little, but I do love rain. I find it comforting," smiled Deborah.

"It's interesting what we find comforting. I grew up here in the San Fernando Valley, and I love the sound of air conditioning," admitted Kimberly with a chuckle.

"I'm glad we were able to get together finally. I guess you heard I had a run-in with Dee?"

"I did, it's hard not to hear the gossip in a place like SMDC. Are you okay?"

"Yes, I'm fine, but she caught me off guard, she was so angry," said Deborah sadly.

"I don't know her well, but she does seem a little uptight," agreed Kimberly. "Do you want to talk about it? I mean, we listen to other people all the time, but it's so important that we take care of ourselves and each other too."

"Thank you." Deborah appreciated the offer to unload in a safe place. "I knew there would be office politics, and there are always personalities to get to know when you come to a new place, but... I guess I was shocked that someone who supposedly understands people could be so off? Maybe she was having a bad day."

"That's very generous of you." Kimberly thought for a moment, then said, "I think it's like this: Dee is very old school, she went to Northwestern University and studied psychology with old-time professors who held Freud and his type up as gods, and they kind of look down on us amateurs for coming in with our new ideas. I think maybe she is a little threatened by you? You are young enough to be her daughter, and you have had some good successes in your short time here?"

"Thank you, but I still find it hard to understand

why she would be so resistant to something that works?"

Kimberly paused for a minute. "I am studying to be an NLP Therapist, it's a very new approach to psychotherapy and Dee isn't too impressed with it or me either!

"What's NLP?"

"It stands for Neuro-Linguistic Programming, it was developed back in the 70s and is just catching on now.. You're familiar with CBT?"

"Yeah, it was just becoming popular in the UK before I left."

"Ok, well, CBT is good, but it has its limitations; it deals with conscious thoughts, reframing them and all that. Well, NLP deals with the subconscious, it has many techniques to help the client get to the unconscious source of the problem. All feelings and emotions are driven by the unconscious mind, that's where the problems are, so reframing thoughts is kinda, well a bit late in my opinion!"

"I always thought that. I mean, if you've already had the thought, what's the point in reframing it? The horse is out of the box, so to speak. What's the point of giving him a new name while you are chasing him around the paddock, trying to get him back in the box?!" laughed Deborah.

"Exactly! You can't put the toothpaste back in the tube! But seeing your own old ideas is hard. Sometimes we need a little help. I think it was Galileo who said you cannot teach a man anything, you can only help him find it within himself."

Deborah laughed again, "Listen to you, did you just get the Discovery Channel?"

Kimberly smiled. "Don't be too impressed, I have been helping my son with a science project... Maybe you and Dee should talk?"

"Are you serious? I doubt she will ever want to

speak to me again, did you hear what she called me?!"

"I know, but she is scared. She is retiring soon, and her life is about to change dramatically."

"I would love to talk to her, but I doubt very much if she would be open to listening to me," sighed Deborah, shaking her head. "You weren't there."

"I know, but maybe you just need to listen to her?"

Deborah paused for a moment and saw how she had fallen into a familiar trap of thinking she needed to be the one to fix and teach and rescue.

"Wow! I just had a thought, and it struck me as so funny!" Deborah was laughing out loud at herself.

"Do share?" begged Kimberly amused.

"Teach and Rescue," replied Deborah. "You know, like Search and Rescue! It's my shtick, I do it all the time, I see what's wrong with someone, and then I teach and rescue them!"

"That's funny," laughed Kimberly. "Yes, but, that's what *you* think is wrong with them?"

"Yikes! I am so arrogant, I always think I know what the other person needs!"

"Okay don't go overboard!"

The next day Deborah got a call from Dee.

"I want to apologize for what I said yesterday." She spoke sternly catching Deborah off guard.

"Thank you, I appreciate that." Deborah paused, knowing it couldn't have been easy for Dee to call. She was the professional, the one with all the credentials and textbook training, and here she was, apologising to the new girl for her behaviour.

"Would you like to talk sometime?" inquired Deborah, she thought this might be the only time Dee would be open to the offer and so she took the chance.

"Uh, yes," mumbled Dee hesitantly. "I'm just surprised you would want to talk to me after the way I was so unprofessional yesterday?"

"We've never gotten a chance to get to know each other, so maybe this is a good time? How about coffee, your place or mine?"

The next evening Deborah sat on her deck overlooking the canal, waiting for Dee to arrive. She soaked up the warm evening air and waved to Sheldon as he took his evening walk with Jennifer. Deborah hoped that the scent from the jasmine and the twinkle of the moonlight on the water would help keep things calm.

"Thank you again for meeting me. I can't apologize enough for the very unprofessional way I acted," announced Dee uncomfortably, wondering where to put herself.

"It's okay, we all have our off days."

"Yes, but I just don't know what happened. I have been in analysis for years, and it's very rare for my anger to show itself like that. I have made an appointment with my analyst to do some extra intensive work, so don't worry, it won't happen again."

"Ok, but maybe there's another way?" hinted Deborah cautiously.

"What do you mean?"

"Well, if you have been trying something for a long time and it's not working..."

"Oh no, analysis works very well, I was just...overtired from traveling and...you know, there's no excuse, no excuse," insisted Dee, shaking her head and smiling forcefully.

"You said something that I found very interesting. You said something like, no one can just decide to be happy? Why not?"

Dee looked at Deborah cautiously, "What do you mean? I mean, it's the subconscious, you can't just ignore it, denial never works, it will just come out at you from another angle if you do that. We always need to get to the subconscious root of our anger."

"I see… Well, actually, I don't," replied Deborah gently. "I have never been to analysis, but when you are working with your analyst, does it make you feel better to keep going over the past?"

Dee laughed, "Functional Analysis isn't about feeling better, it's about getting to roots and causes in the subconscious. Going to the dentist doesn't feel good, but it's necessary."

"Ok, but no one goes to the dentist for twenty years to work on the same tooth. Surely someone who did that would either be a masochist or need to get a better dentist?"

Dee paused. "Okay, so maybe that wasn't a good analogy. But what you young people don't seem to understand is the need for functional assessment of the subconscious to determine the factors that cause and maintain problem behavior, and that doesn't always feel…good."

"But why would you keep digging around in the subconscious if it makes you or your clients leave feeling bad?" responded Deborah, hoping it wasn't going to lead to another outburst.

"Nobody wants them to feel bad, it's about working at how to correct old behaviors. Looking at your past, 'digging around in the subconscious,' as you put it, is the best way to understand why we behave the way we do now."

"Are you asking me or telling me?" inquired Deborah.

"Uh? Look, it's what I was taught by the top professors in the field of psychology, and I have based my practice on this for over thirty years! You can't just decide to be happy."

"Sorry, but it just doesn't make sense to me.

People come to us for help, and surely we should be offering them more than just coping and correcting? I admit I only know a little about the history of Psychology, and I'm sure you know a lot more, but I just can't believe at the core of our beings we are dark, savage beasts who need to be tamed and contained. I believe we are all amazing, resilient, spiritual souls, pure love that can shine in the face of tragedy and mediocrity alike?"

Dee didn't respond, she sat there thinking. Deborah could sense a slight drop in her defenses, so she continued. "If you were to put your hand in a fire, your natural reaction is to take it out. Our inherent nature tells us to. Isn't going back into the pain of the past over and over like going against nature? That same nature that tells you to stop hurting yourself with the fire? Enough already, as you Americans say!"

Dee thought for a moment. "Okay, so you have your way of working, and I have mine. We all have our own truth."

"Yes, we do. We are all living in our own truth, our own thought-created reality," offered Deborah with a big sigh.

Dee looked at her curiously for a moment and then suddenly got up. She clearly had had enough, she had listened as much as she could, and now it was time to go.

"Thank you for meeting me, and I hope we can continue to work together...like real professionals," concluded Dee.

"Sure," agreed Deborah, smiling.

Dee looked at her as if to say, stop being so nice, then she turned and left.

"Kimberly, I don't think I listened very well. It was so hard not to put my point across."

"Don't worry. Remember, we are all doing the best we can!"

18
Austin and Chicago

1996

"Deborah, we need you to have a meeting with the Director, Nora Ephron. She's in from New York and staying at the Beverly Wilshire. She's never made a movie with special effects before so you are going to need to hold her hand. John Travolta is going to play the angel and you are going to have to explain to her how these fake wings of yours are going to be convincing."

Deborah had heard of Nora Ephron, about how she had worked her way up to be one of the most respected women in Hollywood. She had been married to either Woodward or Bernstein, the journalists who broke the Watergate scandal, and was now writing and directing big, successful movies. Deborah ran straight out to the video store to rent the film that was made about their relationship. If they are going to make a movie about your life, thought Deborah, it's not bad having Meryl Streep play you and Jack Nicholson play your husband!

Deborah was so excited, this was just what she had hoped and worked for. *Babe* was a big hit by now and getting awards, and as she was the only one in LA who had worked on the animatronics, she was in high demand. It was great to be working on any movie, but to be part of what she called the "grown ups," the supervisors and producer types, meant she had made it. She arrived at the Beverly Wilshire and as the valet guy drove her little, black car away, she stepped past the doorman of the very grand hotel. The Beverly Wilshire had been used in many movies, so it was all feeling a bit surreal as she got into the elevator to go up to the Penthouse suite.

Nora and her sister, Deliah, welcomed her in and ordered room service. They discussed the wings that Deborah and her team were going to make to turn John Travolta into the Archangel Michael, only this Michael was going to be a hung-over slob. Deborah drew pictures and explained how each of the different sets of wings would attach. Nora had some clear ideas of what she wanted but had no idea how they were going to make it look real.

"That's my job," assured Deborah, and she shared a line she had learned from Sue, "The impossible, we can do today, the really impossible will have to wait till tomorrow."

The first time she met John was at his home in the elite neighbourhood just above Sunset Boulevard, overlooking Beverly Hills. It was a lovely house, full of beautiful things like you would see in a magazine about movie stars' homes, but it really felt like a home, lived in by a real family. John wasn't at home when they arrived, so they were invited to set up the wings in the living room and told he would be there very soon. She was just about to open the front door to go out to the car again as John opened the door to come in. Her heart jumped! She was inviting John Travolta, the star of movies she had swooned over as a young girl, into his own home! His eyes were so dreamy blue and he gave her a huge grinning smile at the irony of the situation. Her heart fluttered like a teenager as she stepped outside to catch her breath. *How was this happening?* She felt a huge surge of gratitude go from her toes right up to her heart. The fitting went really well, John was as excited as they were to be doing this, and made it fun for everyone while at the same time making a fuss of his gorgeous wife, who was trying on designer gowns for the Golden Globes that was happening in a few days' time.

Deborah informed Bob that she would be away for a few months filming and hoped that would give them all time for things to cool down. Going on location was always a treat at the end of the long hours and weeks designing and building the effects and this time it was Austin, Texas, with a few weeks in Chicago at the end. Austin was a very cool city, but she soon discovered it wasn't anything like the rest of Texas. It was trendy and full of bars and students, whereas the rest of Texas was, well *very* Southern Bible Beltish. When they went out into the neighbouring countryside to film, there was nothing as far as the eye could see except endless fields of cows and a church in every direction. They just happened to be there during the South by Southwest music festival, so the town was even more alive with music than usual. The first Sunday afternoon she went out to explore, she could hear a live outdoor concert happening. She followed the music and stumbled on Iggy Pop doing a live gig on a massive stage right in the middle of the street! She was having a blast hanging out with Nora and the other actors. The memories of all that pain, the violence, and the living nightmare that seemed like it would never end were long gone. She hardly even thought of it anymore and when she did, she just pushed those thoughts out of her head. When she wasn't needed on set, she would find a quiet place and read more of Father Thomas's book that she borrowed from Carol, trying her best to get these new ideas into her head.

John was at least six feet tall, so the wings needed

very large white feathers to make a wingspan that could possibly lift him up. There are no white birds with three-foot feathers in the world, and if there were, they weren't going to let some crazy movie people have them. Deborah and her team had sculpted and produced fake, plastic feathers for the tips of the wings, and blended them in with white turkey and chicken feathers for the top, which would be blended onto John's back. The tops of the wings also had to contain mechanisms that would make them move slightly as if they were real. This all meant that the folded wings would go almost down to John's ankles and, as anyone knows, when you walk downstairs with a long coat on, the coat will drag on the stairs behind you. Deborah knew this would be a problem as John's first hero shot was to be him coming down wooden stairs. She told Nora and the 1st AD several times that the plastic feathers would catch on the steps, but they kept saying, "*Don't worry, they look amazing!!*"

The day arrived to shoot John's first big entrance. Studio heads from LA had flown in and were all sitting in their director's chairs along with Nora and Deliah, waiting to see Deborah's amazing wings, as she stood behind them, praying that it would be okay.

"Action!" shouted Nora, and John started to slump his way down the stairs. CRASH, CRASH, CRASH! went the fabricated feathers on the step behind him! All of a sudden there was an uproar. "*DEBORAH!!*" screamed Nora at the top of her voice, as the sound man came running in to see what had blown his earphones off, while John was now shouting, "*NORA, DEBORAH!*"

Deborah wanted to run and hide, but she stepped forward, her heart pounding. There was no way to say, "I told you so" in front of the forty people now staring at her. "Fix it, *now,*" demanded Nora sternly, knowing she had not listened but unable to lose face in front of her producers and crew. Deborah took John off to the side and took the wings off and with a pair of scissors, cut four inches out of the middle of the wings and lifted them up with safety pins. Weeks of careful work blending real feathers in with the fabricated ones to cover up the mechanisms was trashed and redone in five minutes.

"Hurry up!" urged the 1st AD. "Thousands of dollars are pouring through the air while you fix that!"

Deborah wanted to scream, she wondered why she didn't work in an office or a supermarket bagging groceries, it would be a lot less trouble. They shot the scene again and nothing more was said about it, but months later, when Deborah saw the finished movie at the cast and crew screening back in LA, she swore she could see the safety pins.

Things smoothed over and the filming continued. Everyone became friends again helped by John's amazing ability to put everyone at ease. He was brilliant at remembering everyone's names, even the caterer and transport guys, signing autographs for the locals after long days on his feet and making everyone feel special. Nora soon forgot about the snafu and welcomed Deborah's advice for the rest of filming. It was a glorious few months hanging out with her and the other actors. Oscar winner William Hurt often sat with her for lunch, and she became good friends with the costume designer, hanging out together in the evenings.

For one particular scene, John needed to fight with a bull in a field on the distant horizon. The bull was an animatronic that had been made by her colleagues, but it required her to stand alone with John off in the distance to set up the wings, and then run out of shot when she heard *action* on her radio. This took all morning and as they chatted in between takes, John started to design an outfit for Deborah to wear.

"I think you would look good in some kind of Mary Quant get up, you know, sixties style," imagincd John as he got ready for another charge at the bull.

"If I wore that, would you dance with me?" asked Deborah cheekily.

"Honey, I would dance with you anytime, but not now!"

"*Action!*" shouted Nora over the radio, and he ran off at full speed toward the raging fake bull.

Deborah couldn't believe she had just asked him to dance with her, but didn't think any more of it until about two weeks later when they were doing a night shoot. The scene called for John to dance with the actress playing a waitress, and Deborah was ready with extra feathers to throw on the floor where they would be dancing. The sound guy was playing the music on some speakers so John could get the timing right and the crew were all standing around waiting, waiting, waiting, like film crews always do. 'Hurry up and wait' is just the way movies are made.

"Now!" instructed John, turning to Deborah and stretching out his hand.

"What?" Deborah, looked around confused.

"Dance! We are going to dance, now."

She couldn't believe it, here she was in a field in Southern Texas, in the middle of the night, being asked to dance by John Travolta!

Deborah's heart jumped, she dropped the feathers she had been holding in her hand and stepped forward in disbelief. He pointed to the sound guy, who pressed play, and he led her on to the makeshift dance floor, the crew all watching in admiration. It was the most divine few minutes of her life as he gently placed his hand on her waist and twirled her around, she gasped and laughed and everyone applauded. It was magical, she felt like Princess Diana when she had danced with John at the White House.

They moved to Chicago for last few weeks of shooting, which was quite an adjustment after being out in the fields of Texas for months. Chicago was loud and busy, the tall 1930s buildings following the river as it snaked through downtown was enchanting. It reminded her of Manchester, but much grander. They were treated to a trip up to the very top of the Sears Tower above the tourist observation deck to the maintenance roof for another thrill of a lifetime. The next day the venerable movie director Robert Altman came to visit Nora, so they stopped filming for them to have an impromptu chat. Finally, it was the last day of shooting for Deborah. She and John were wrapped a few days before the rest of the cast and crew, as there was no Angel in the last few scenes that were left to shoot. It was another night shoot and, as Hollywood tradition goes, no matter what time you start work, breakfast is always served first. The breakfast truck was parked outside a vintage poster shop on a Chicago side street under the L train, and as the crew lined up in the drizzling rain for their breakfast burritos and bagels, William Hurt tapped her on the shoulder.

"I saw this and had to get it for you." He handed her a large cardboard tube. Deborah was confused, she said thank you and went to their special effects truck to put down her burrito and take a look. It was a poster. It was a poster of her favourite movie! It was *Breakfast at Tiffany's*, in Italian!! She fought back the tears as she flashed back to that grey day in Manchester, staring out the window, wondering how people managed to live their lives, unable to think of anything outside the prison she had created for herself with her own thoughts. And yet, here she was, living an amazing life. *Maybe this is what looking inside for happiness looks like*, she wondered. When you stop looking in the wrong direction, beautiful things just show up!

Deborah and John's last scene was finished at about 3 a.m., and after the customary applause as she and John took a bow, the crew broke for "lunch." She felt sad as she packed away all the wings, tools, and supplies to be shipped back to LA, but it was a good sad; it had been an amazing experience that had come to an end, and she felt good to be able to feel the feelings and not be panicked by them. She went to find Nora to say goodbye and thank you.

"I'm wrapped," announced Deborah sadly, as she sat down next to Nora, who was eating her lunch with Deliah and William Hurt.

"Oh my goodness," said Nora jumping up, "Don't leave yet, I'll be right back!" as she ran off into the night. Everyone was a little taken aback as Nora was not the kind of person to *jump* anywhere. She was your classic New York Princess and had plenty of people around to do everything and anything for her. She came back a few minutes later with a gift and a big hug for Deborah. "Just a little something to say thank you. If you ever need anything, *please* let me know."

"Aw, you didn't have to!" offered Deborah, absolutely thrilled that Nora had thought of her.

As she sat on her hotel bed an hour or so later, she opened up the present. It was a little book by an old friend of Nora's called *Love, Loss and What I Wore*. It was an adorable memoir with little drawings of the outfits this lady wore at each memorable occasion in her life. Her Bat Mitzvah dress, her graduation gown, her wedding dress, what she wore to the hospital when her son was born, what she wore to the divorce signing and what she wore to the Copacabana to see Dean

Martin and Jerry Lewis the night she stole an ashtray. As she flipped through the pages a handwritten card fell out.

Nora Ephron
(the Ephron had a line drawn through)

You were the angel behind the wings!
Thank you for everything. I know you are going
to have a brilliant future
Nora.

19
El Segundo

1997

A week after she got back it was arranged that Deborah would continue with Anton. Deborah had mixed feelings about this. She was very keen to be working with him - here was something new, a young man, a veteran - but she was also nervous about what it would mean for her relationship with Dee and her place at SMDC. The last thing she wanted was to bump into Dee with Anton and for everyone to feel uncomfortable, so she asked Bob if they could meet at his place, at least the first few times.

A couple of days later, Deborah arrived at Bob's house in El Segundo just south of LAX airport, further down the long line of Los Angeles beaches. It was about fifteen minutes in the car, a drive which Deborah always loved. It was fun to drive under the approaching Jumbo Jets that seemed to be almost landing on the roof of her car. The sound of the Rolls Royce jet engines roaring so close over her head was a thrill, especially if she got the timing just right to be stopped at the traffic lights at Lincoln and Sepulveda.

Anton was already there drinking a cup of coffee with Bob in the kitchen.

"I need to go out, but my wife, Veronica, is in her office, through there, so you guys can hang out in here if you like. Help yourselves to whatever and just give her a shout when you leave."

"Thanks, Bob!" They sat down at the kitchen table, and Deborah asked Anton how he was doing.

"I have...well, to tell the truth, I was totally mixed up after we talked last time, but what I kept remembering was how much we laughed. I feel...well, calm, and I haven't felt like that in years."

"Yes, it's so good to laugh," admitted Deborah, smiling. "It's well-documented as being a great natural healing power. Letting it all out like that is very life-affirming and puts you in touch with your sense of wellbeing. I'm guessing you don't laugh too much?"

Anton lowered his head and with a big sigh, mumbled, "No, my life has been one crappy thing after another. I grew up out in San Bernardino County, my mother died when I was a kid, so my childhood was rough, being tossed around the family like a hot potato. Then came the foster homes, it was like being in a game of roulette, never knowing where I was gonna land next! Landing on Red meant getting smacked upside the head, and Black meant nothing to eat. I thought going into the Military would give me a place to belong, but then I lost all the guys in my unit out in the Gulf and the only people I really talk to these days just want to keep reminding me about it all."

Deborah's heart went out to this young man who was trying so hard to understand.

"So, what I have learned for myself is that I'm okay right here, right now, it's all any of us have."

"Sure," agreed Anton, "It's safe and okay here in Bob's kitchen, but what about when I get home?"

"Uh, hold on, where did you just go?" asked Deborah with a little sarcasm.

"What do you mean?" Anton looked around himself as if he were suddenly invisible.

"Well, we were both sitting here on this really nice Thursday morning in El Segundo, and you went off into Thursday afternoon, to your apartment somewhere in...Westchester? You thought about later on today and with that thought came some uncomfortable feelings, so now you are feeling bad about a time in the future that hasn't even happened yet? It's like you have time-travel superpowers! Oh my gosh, Anton, are you a Timelord?!" alleged Deborah, joking around.

Anton laughed nervously and then sighed heavily again. "No, I mean I'm okay when I'm here, but not when I'm there."

"Of course not, there is only here! Trying to be in two places at once is going to make anyone feel a bit squirmy. I used to be a great time traveler, my thoughts were always off into tomorrow or yesterday, and so a mentor once asked me to look at my feet when my thinking went off into outer space. Look down at your feet, Anton, go on, look down at your feet right now." Anton didn't understand but looked down at his bare feet in his Surf Shop sandals. "I was told to always have my thinking in the same place as my feet. Right now my feet are under Bob's kitchen table where I'm talking to you, and that's where my thinking needs to be, in our conversation right here, right?" Anton looked up and down for a minute. "It's very easy to go off into next week or yesterday so when I catch myself doing that, I start to look down at my feet, remind myself I only have right here, right now, and I just seem to lose interest in those other thoughts."

"Okay, maybe." Anton shrugged his shoulders.

"When my mentor first suggested all this to me, it felt very threatening," admitted Deborah. "It was like she was saying, it didn't hurt or it didn't happen or I should get over it! And I was like, hey! It did hurt, it did happen, and I can't get over it!! I'd gotten so used to watching and rewatching those movies in my head about what had happened to me that they had become part of me. I thought if I let go of these, then who am

I? And that was very scary!"

"Yeah, I feel a bit like you are asking me to jump off a cliff," agreed Anton nervously.

"Sure, I felt like that too, but I was so sick of my old life, so tired of trying and then trying again and getting nowhere, that I was willing to let go purely out of exhaustion, but I just didn't know how to do it. I felt exactly like you said, at the edge of a cliff, being asked to jump off and not knowing how to do it. I just wanted the pain in my head to go away. Tell me what to do, I told her. Where do I go? What do I wear?! Arghhh!!" Deborah flung her arms in the air as if she was drowning.

"So, how did you do it?" Anton was still feeling cautious.

"Hmmm...you know, it's funny, I remember being on the phone with Shelly saying all that and feeling quite panicked, or was it excitement? Hard to tell sometimes, anyway, then I remember a few days later I realized I was ok. I probably put the phone down and just got on with whatever I was supposed to, I don't know, maybe I did the dishes or just went to bed. But looking back I just stopped paying attention to the thoughts, and slowly the horrible memories lost their hold on me. I can still remember everything clearly about the muggings and the violence, but it just doesn't hurt or scare me anymore. Weird, eh?"

"Yeah, very weird," agreed Anton. He thought for a few moments. "I could see how that might work for someone else, but my stuff is so...there's just so much of it...this is going to take a long time, I'm just not like you? Besides, they tell me now that I have *complex* PTSD!"

Deborah paused for a moment, she recognized the wall of resistance that Anton could see as real, but that she knew was just made of old ideas, so she plowed right through it.

"You are a surfer, right? And you like good music, right? And don't you work at that really cool computer store on 3rd Street Promenade? You must know a lot about computers?"

"Yeah, I learned computers in the Military, but that just makes me a nerd with no friends, and as for surfing, well...to be honest...I, uh...I've never actually gone out...in the waves, that is."

"But you have all the gear, and you talked about how cool it is?"

"Yeah, but I just sit on my board and watch them...I'm too...I can't believe I'm admitting this, but this Marine Sergeant is scared. Besides they have always told me if I went under, it would trigger all my Gulf War stuff, the panic of being trapped, that I'm not ready to handle that yet. What if I get sucked under? It can happen, you know."

Deborah tried to hide her sadness at how much this young man had been held back by the old ideas other people had put to him.

"Yes, I know but that's kind of normal; I would feel panicked too if I fell off and got sucked under! Anyone would, but we all fall off our "boards" sometimes, and besides, the rest of the time it looks like so much fun! I know there are classes, let's find you a cool dude surfing teacher who can show you how to do it right, and as for being a computer nerd, I heard there are some pretty cool, not to mention very rich billionaire computer nerds out there who are married to amazing women and having a great time!"

"I don't know," Anton hesitated.

"Well, I do!" insisted Deborah, hoping her confidence would rub off. "How about it?" and stood up to show him that she meant business. "This is so exciting. See you next week!"

Anton left not knowing quite what just happened, and Deborah popped her head around the door of

Veronica's office.

"Hey, V, how are you?"

"Hey! So nice to see you again. How did it go? Oops, not supposed to ask that."

"Good, I hope. What are you working on?"

"Oh, just going over the budget for a Nintendo commercial, we start shooting Monday. Hey, are you on a movie right now?"

"No, I was supposed to start one last week, but it's being put back a month as the Production Designer is working out some new ideas, why?"

"Well, my Production Coordinator just let me down big-time and hey, you could do it!"

"Don't be ridiculous! Remember me, I'm the one who does animatronics, visual effects, I don't know anything about Production!"

"Yes you do, you know what a Call Sheet is and all the equipment and all the crew. Production is just about getting it all to the right places at the right time, and you seem very good at that," persisted Veronica, putting her 'pretty please, please, please' face on. "My Production Manager, Victoria, will tell you what to do, and I'll tell her to be nice to you. It's just a one-day shoot, and we will have sooooo much fun!"

"V, you know this is why they call you a female bulldozer, right?"

Veronica turned back to her computer, "Calling Victoria now, she'll let you know everything. Byeeeee!"

The following Sunday Deborah had gone out with Abby, they had been to a movie and had something to eat at The Soup Plantation after. She had just got home when the phone rang.

"Put the TV on!" cried Abby.

"Why, what's going on?"

"Princess Diana just died!"

"Don't be ridiculous," scolded Deborah.

It was about 11 p.m., and Deborah switched on her TV to see the most extraordinary sight. Every Channel was showing a British reporter. She flipped from NBC to CBS to Fox News. ITV, BBC, and Channel 4 reporters were everywhere! Deborah felt very strange for a moment. She was in her house in the Venice Canals in California, and yet her TV was all British!

"What happened?" Deborah couldn't believe her eyes

"I don't know. Speak to you tomorrow," mumbled Abby and hung up.

Deborah couldn't believe what she was seeing, as she watched the events unfold. She had never really been bothered either way about having a Royal family, they were just always there. She remembered as a little girl being very disappointed when she realised that her mum wasn't going to get a turn at being the Queen. Deborah suddenly felt very far from home, very...British. It was late, and eventually, she fell asleep. The next few days were very odd, the news about Princess Diana's death was everywhere, and she felt strangely drawn to watch the drama unfold. It was the only time in her life she actually felt homesick and was acutely aware that the Americans around her, although very moved and fascinated, just didn't get it.

Thursday came, and as Deborah drove into the tunnel under LAX on her drive to Bob's house, she got an eerie feeling. It looked just like the tunnel in Paris where Diana's car had smashed into the wall. She shuddered and realized she needed to stop watching so much news. Deborah arrived first this time, Anton was about 20 minutes late. He was quite a respectful young man, his military training still part of his life, so Deborah was curious about what had happened.

"Uh, sorry," apologised Anton catching his breath as he came in through the screen door. "The waves were perfect this morning, and I wanted to catch just one more." His shirt was still wet and his eyes were red from the salty ocean water.

"Uh, so I guess you found a teacher?" inquired Deborah trying to hide her surprise.

"Yeah, Alfie, he's really great, he had me up on the board the first morning, and we have been out every day since. It's so cool, I even get the surf report faxed to my apartment now so I can see what the waves are like as soon as I get up, like all the other surf guys!"

"That's amazing, Anton! You sound like you are enjoying it?" ventured Deborah, a little bemused.

"Yes, Alfie says I'm a natural, but it'll be a long time till I can do what he does. He goes to Hawaii and Fiji, and next week he's going to take me down to Huntington Beach with him!" Anton went on about waves and boards and the guys, board wax and competitions, longboards, shortboards, and board shorts. "I got a pretty bad cut yesterday on my leg, but Alfie says it's just one of those things."

"This is great!" cried Deborah. "Not the cut, I mean, you are doing really well. And how is work?"

"Oh, pretty chilled. Some of the guys came into the shop and I was able to help them out with a good deal on some game stuff that they wanted so my boss was pleased with the extra sales and the dudes at the beach think I'm cool for hooking them up with the right computer gear."

"So, an average week then?" acknowledged Deborah, trying not to smile too much at this transformation. Anton laughed and told a few more stories about the dudes and the waves. He was clearly having a great time. She didn't want to be too skeptical and thought maybe he should slow down, but today he was just enjoying the ride.

The following Tuesday evening Deborah got a call from Anton, his voice was trembling.

"Debs, can we talk?"

"Sure, Anton, what's the matter?"

"I just got some really bad news," groaned Anton, sounding like his old, anxious self.

"I'm so sorry, what happened?"

"Alfie is moving...he's leaving LA."

Deborah could feel his sadness oozing down the phone.

"Oh, I'm so sorry, you must be really disappointed..."

There was a long, painful silence, and then Anton said, "This always happens to me. People always leave, or I have to leave, or something always gets messed up, and I'm on my own again. This is why I don't get involved with anyone; whenever I let anyone in, I lose them and it just brings back all the pain of losing my buddies in the Gulf... When I was on active duty it became routine, you got close to the guys in your unit, your life depended on it. It depended on us being so close we could read each other's minds, and then BOOM they would be dead, gone, and I'd be on my own again. One moment your buddy is there and then his body is in pieces, gone. It happened over and over...but I thought back here it would be different, that people would stick around. But they don't, they just up and leave! My ex-wife, gone, Alfie, gone. I can't keep anyone in my life...my life is a mess."

"And what am I?" asked Deborah gently, "chopped liver? .... I'm here Anton, I didn't go anywhere." She couldn't see Anton's face but hoped he smiled a little. "I'm here, your job is still here, your other friends at the beach, your roommate, and the guys at the VA are all still here, right?" Deborah knew that painful void too well where life is like a black hole and it seems there is no way out.

After a long silence, Anton mumbled, "Yeah, I guess."

"I know you are hurting right now and it seems to have brought up all the other times you feel you were left on your own, but right here right now you are really okay. All those other times are memories, they are in the past, they can't hurt you in this moment right here. Anton, where are your feet?"

"On the ends of my legs."

Deborah laughed, "Good one! No wonder the guys at the beach like to hang out with you, you are too funny!"

"Yeah but..."

"No buts," interrupted Deborah. "You have the free will to ignore those thoughts, don't get sucked back into the story... When you are out in the water, do you take every wave that comes?"

"No, that would be suicide."

"Well, it's like that with thinking. Sometimes I can be walking on the beach having a good time with a friend, and suddenly I get a thought like, *kill yourself now*. Just like that, from nowhere it seems. Before it would have scared me - Holy Moly, I am going crazy again! But now I understand that it's just an old habit that is slowly dying of neglect, and I ignore it. I don't have to listen to it. If I don't take it seriously, it fades away. In fact, I haven't had one of those thoughts in a long time. I might want to kill other people sometimes but not myself much anymore."

"But we were having such a good time," mumbled Anton.

"I know, but do you see how once that idea of being alone again came into your head, which isn't even true, the special effects department in your mind went into overdrive to make it seem like it was, and then dug through all the old files to bring up all the evidence to make you feel lousy? You then noticed that you felt lousy and thought some more crappy thoughts. That's how we get messed up. Do that for too long, and the men in white coats come and take us away."

There was silence.

"You still there, Anton?" Deborah could hear him breathing but wanted to keep the connection going.

"Yes. I think I just realised something... It's like we are all living in our own video game. Only it was me who wrote the software for mine?"

"Yes, exactly! That's brilliant! We are all living in our own video game created by our own thinking! And if you are the one writing the software and it's not working, then change it. I don't know all the right lingo, but I think if there are bugs in the system, wouldn't you dump that file and write a new one?"

"I guess. But my mind isn't a computer, I can't just delete files. You have to have serious electric shock treatment for that!"

"Okay, but when you have lots of programs open on your computer and several of them aren't responding, and you are wondering hey, where is that music coming from? Then you know it's not being used well, right? When you are up on your board and it's just you riding that glorious wave, I bet you don't remember in that moment all the times you fell off, right? Or how scared you were to even try? In fact, that would probably make you fall off!! You are in the moment, you are in the zone. That doesn't mean you never fell off before or that you won't again. But in that zone moment, you are one with the wave and all those other times are irrelevant." Deborah couldn't believe she was using surfing and computers, two things she knew very little about, to get the ideas over.

"I guess," admitted Anton, slowly coming around.

"Besides, you could go visit Alfie and hang out with him as a friend!"

"He moved to Huntington Beach to start a surf School down there."

"What?! I thought you were going to say he moved to Hawaii or Bondi Beach on the other side of the world! Huntington is only what, 30 miles down the coast? You could go on your day off!!" Deborah bit her lip so as not to say more on the drama that Anton had created in his head.

"Anton, I always used to think that it was outside stuff that could make me happy or sad. I thought I had to have everything worked out and going smoothly before I could feel okay, the problem was that it was so painful waiting for all those people and situations to be just how I needed, that I never felt okay. Now I see I was always looking in the wrong direction for happiness. It comes from inside, it's that thing you get when you catch the wave and you are in the moment. Eventually, I got to see I can be okay even when things don't go my way, that things out there can fall apart but I don't have to!"

"But that goes against everything I have ever been told!"

"I guess, but do you see it could be true for you? I saw you last week, so excited, so alive and loving life. It's not a theory I made up, I saw you with my own eyes having a great time, having friends and a good life just like anyone else. I don't know why all those other professional mental health types like to keep dragging up the past and analyzing it...if you open the fridge and something smells bad, throw it out! Who cares if it's the chicken or the fish!"

There was a long silence.

"How are you feeling now, Anton?"

"Okay, I guess."

Deborah smiled, "Okay is pretty good and quite

understandable in the situation. You are disappointed, and that's normal... Hey, you know how a piano has black and white keys?" Anton mumbled a yes. "Well let's say the white ones are happy and the black ones are sad. You need both of them to make music... I love your idea that we are all living in our own video game, now it's up to you to design a new one. Spend the next couple of days watching what comes up. I bet you will see that it's actually okay to feel a bit down sometimes, it means you are human, it's just part of the music. Anton, it's normal and nothing to be afraid of, trust me. See you Thursday."

20
San Francisco

Deborah had been thinking a lot about a conversation she had had with Shelly almost ten years earlier. It just kept popping into her mind and was hard to ignore. They had talked about how different people have different ideas about who God is and how it doesn't make any difference to God.

"Abby, do you believe in God?"

"Wow, what brought that on?" Deborah was away on location in San Francisco and just wanted to hear a familiar voice on the phone. "Are you okay?"

"Yeah, totally fine, I've just been thinking about it a lot recently, that's all."

Deborah was working on a remake of the classic movie *Dr. Dolittle* with Eddie Murphy. She had been hired to make a life-size tiger and a dog. The movie was full of animals, so she and her colleagues had been working non-stop for months. The real tiger, Jake, lived on an animal reservation called Shambala, owned by the actress Tippi Hedron, star of the Hitchcock movie *The Birds*. It was just north of LA in the Mojave Desert, and she had enjoyed spending a lot of time there with this majestic animal, copying his every detail. Back at the film studio in LA, she had had one of the most satisfying moments of her career.

Every day during filming a movie, the director, producers, and heads of departments all watch the footage from the day before. They are looking for any mistakes so that they can do a reshoot straight away if needed. It would cost a fortune to bring everyone back months later, so watching the "Dailies," as they are called, was always done at lunch the following day. The director had invited some bigwig studio head to come and see how it was going, and as her tiger was in these particular shots, Deborah had been invited to join them. The director, visitor, producers, and DP were sitting in the front row of the screening room at CBS Radford Studios, and Deborah, the costume designer, script supervisor, and 1st AD were all sat behind. As they watched and ate their boxed lunches, the director explained the story and chatted with the visitor.

"Ah, but you see this is the problem when you work with real animals!" announced the visitor confidently, "You can always tell where the animal trainer is hiding. He's just there, see, off camera making noises or holding some chicken or whatever they do to get the animal's attention, see? The animal is always looking for his trainer and not directly at the actor or the camera, it's a challenge."

Deborah's stomach made a little flip, they were all looking at her animatronic puppet!! The visitor had been fooled into thinking it was the real tiger! Her colleagues in the back row gave her air high fives, and she felt ecstatic.

After the movie was finished shooting, she settled back into her regular schedule in LA, seeing clients and hanging out with her friends. Anton was still doing well, and Kristi had made herself indispensable in her work with Dr. Saunders. With the invention of email, she was able to reconnect with her old mentor,

Shelly, back in London, and share her adventures, triumphs, and her new ideas about how the human mind works. They wrote back and forth about the possibility that some Serendipitous, loving Force had always been shaping her life, and now that she wasn't stuck in her old ideas, she was beginning to see it. Shelly encouraged her to read more and explore new ideas, so she took a stroll up and down the aisle in the Marina Del Rey bookstore. She had read many of the classic self-help books and new-age spirituality books, but nothing had ever grabbed her with any special meaning. She wasn't sure what she wanted, what she was looking for...something real, a place to put her growing thoughts about spirituality. Something must be running the show, she kept thinking, something designed that real tiger, something that magnificent can't just happen. She knew it took a whole team of the most talented people to create a fake one, so maybe there was a Divine Intelligence running the world after all?

As Deborah had gotten to know her neighbours, Sheldon and Jennifer, she had found them more and more fascinating. Sheldon's father was an English Jew, and his mother, a full-blooded Cree Indian. He was a big guy, balding on top, with a ponytail made of his remaining hair. His goatee beard and the combination of being half-Indian made him seem exotic to Deborah's very English eyes. Jennifer was much younger, in her late twenties, an all-American college girl, and the two were devoted to each other. Sheldon often sat on his deck overlooking the canal, smoking his roll-ups and rocking in his favourite chair.

"What's up?" called Sheldon as she passed by on her way back from an evening stroll along the Venice Boardwalk a few days after returning from San

Francisco.

"Hey Sheldon, not much, just thinking."

The setting sun was still warming the air, and the smell of jasmine floated across the water.

"Wanna cup of tea? I have the real English stuff, with milk and two sugars, right?"

Deborah laughed as she stepped up onto their deck and took a seat on the wicker couch next to his rocking chair.

"Jen is inside working on her thesis or dissertation or some paper for college; she works so hard, I only see the back of her head these days. Can't wait for finals to be over and then we can hang out again."

"You two are so cute," complimented Deborah. "I wanted to tell you I have a new client, he's a Veteran too."

"Really? Where did he serve?"

"Gulf War."

"Ah, must be a young kid? They got messed up pretty bad, too."

"Yeah, they had been giving him all this Flooding therapy and it was making him miserable."

Sheldon shook his head.

"Those people don't have a clue. They made me write about all that 'Nam horror and read it out over and over, and all it did was make me crazier. It ruined my first marriage. The flashbacks just got worse, I was like a bear with a sore head on a good day," confessed Sheldon. He leaned forward and lowered his voice. "On the days they made me do that going back and reliving it stuff, I would come home so fired up, so full of anger and rage that I'm sorry to say I took it out on my ex-wife. She would stay away the nights she knew I had had "therapy," and in the end, she just didn't come back." He sat back in his chair as if to say enough said.

"That's awful, I'm so sorry. So what changed? You seem so calm and...together now. I can't imagine you being like that. You and Jennifer have such a great relationship, you're a big teddy bear!"

Sheldon grinned at the compliments.

"Well, after the divorce, I was in a really bad way. I ended up back in the V.A. Hospital for treatment, but I only went on condition they didn't put me through that hell again. So they put me in with this "experimental" group. A young psychologist was trying out some new ideas and, well, it just made so much more sense to me."

Deborah was curious."Ok, I'll bite. What was it?"

"Well, it's not like the other therapies...it's not a therapy actually, no techniques or writing, nothing. This young doctor, who we knew hadn't done any military service, told us that we were all ok, that there was nothing wrong with us, that we were all full of wisdom! We all thought he was full of...well, we thought he was just another "Do Gooder" who would be out of there as soon as a better opportunity came up, but something told me that he really believed it. He really thought we were ok! He kept saying, you are not broken, there is nothing to fix, you just have a whole load of contaminated thinking covering up the wisdom that is in all of us!"

"Wow, ok. So what did he do that changed you?"

"See, that's the amazing thing. He just kept repeating that we were ok, that we didn't need fixing, and some of us started to believe him. He said that it didn't matter what we thought about what had happened to us, more that we understood that it was all just made of thought. We would come out of his sessions feeling ok, and then we just started feeling better, and so we asked for more. I guess it just took the edge off things, I mean all that pressure that I had felt in my head since I got back from 'Nam just wasn't there anymore. I guess I learned not to take all that thinking so seriously."

"Ok, but did he teach you a meditation, tools for how to deal with your thinking? You know, crisis management stuff?" persisted Deborah.

"No. See that's why it's new, it's different. He kept on telling us not to get interested in what we thought about what had happened to us, more important was that we understood that we were the ones doing the thinking. He taught us that there is actually nothing to do. The brain, like the rest of your body, naturally has a self-healing system in it. I'm sure you have learned about the Fight-or-Flight response in your work, right?"

"Yeah, sure."

"So, if you have that going on for too long, you are going to mess yourself up."

"Right, and the stress produces a chemical imbalance, a dysregulation, I've been thinking about that too!"

"But don't you see, the imbalance has only come from the prolonged distressed thinking! We do it to ourselves!" explained Sheldon.

"I know! All those people who are told they have a chemical imbalance and need to be on meds and in therapy for the rest of their lives are doing it to themselves! If they hadn't taken their thinking so seriously, they wouldn't have ended up is such a mess."

Sheldon shrugged his shoulders and gave a 'go figure' kind of look. "Yes, but it's an innocent mistake. I know I did it, and it sounds like you did too?"

"Yes, but we have to tell someone! Why aren't you campaigning in Washington or something?!" pleaded Deborah in frustration.

"Don't get me started," dismissed Sheldon. "Jennifer is writing her paper on it, but it's going to take a while for all those knucklehead doctors to listen and then there are the big Pharma companies who are making billions off of Vets and housewives and stressed-out teenagers who are being fed all those pills. They need us to be ignorant, they are not going to let this get out there. Jen's research is turning up some scary stuff. Look, we do what we can do, and the rest will follow. But that's all science, don't get distracted by the science. The most helpful thing he shared with us was that these thoughts, even the loud ones, even flashbacks, would pass on by whether we ignored them or not, and so by not doing anything with them, our minds calmed down and we felt better, it was that simple."

As Deborah wandered home, she was intrigued. She couldn't get her head around the fact that there was nothing to do. She had known for a long time that she wasn't her thoughts, that ignoring her thoughts was what had helped her and that was certainly better than trying to pour pink paint on them, replace them with positive ones, and she had never got the whole 'reframing' thing, but she suddenly realised that ignoring her thoughts was still *actually doing something*!!! Wow! This blew her mind. All this time she had thought she had found the answer by ignoring her thoughts. Putting them over there in time-out, like naughty children who needed to be scolded and taught a lesson, seemed like such a good idea, but she could see now how that was still putting energy into them! She suddenly saw for herself that that wasn't necessary, that they really would die of neglect just by watching them pass by, as she had suspected. It was as if all that was needed was to become an impartial observer of her thought. Suffering could then be seen with clarity like Frankl had said. Oooh, this was powerful stuff!

A couple of days later, Deborah went to visit Sheldon again; she wanted to know more. She loved chatting with him, he was so calm and funny and had such interesting ideas.

"Can I ask, do you still get flashbacks? Nightmares?"

"I used to, terrible ones. I would wake up screaming, we all went through some terrible stuff out there. But as I started to understand how it all works and that it's not happening right now, that what is in the past can't hurt me, the flashbacks started to come less frequently and the nightmares, they became less frightening. And if I get the occasional one now, I don't freak out, I wait for it to pass. The Shrink told us that everything is made of thought." He sat back in his chair and laughed. "You should have seen the look on our faces when he said that the first time, we thought he was the one who should be in the locked ward!"

"What does that even mean?" Deborah was fascinated.

"Well, we need to be conscious in order to be aware of our thinking, our surroundings right? Well, consciousness is very clever at making those thoughts seem real, like what you do in the movies, it adds in effects, like bringing up feelings and memories, and then adds in some doubt or anxiety. But that is all just made up of thought."

Deborah loved what he was saying, it made so much sense to her.

"Hey, what are you doing Friday night?" inquired Sheldon changing the subject.

"Don't know, why?"

"Well, my son, Sheldon the 3rd is just out of jail, don't ask, anyway they are moving him to a treatment center on Venice Boulevard. It's in a synagogue, or the synagogue is in the treatment center, not quite sure which, but either way, he is there and I thought maybe you would want to come. They do the Friday night service thing, and then we all have dinner, nothing fancy but lots of singing and good company."

"Sure."

Deborah had loved being in the Synagogue that Friday night. She didn't really know much of what was going on, her parents had really never told her much, but she loved the calm feeling she felt there, so she had followed that feeling to find a community of her own. She remembered that conversation with Shelly about Dorothy asking the Tin Man and the Scarecrow for answers, and she realised that maybe she, too, had been looking in the wrong direction for happiness, for connection. She knew it wasn't 'out there,' in a building or a person, but it sure helped to be around people who thought and believed the same way.

On the morning of Saturday, February 2nd, 2003, she sat in Synagogue in Los Angeles. She had found a friendly, new-age kind of spiritual congregation that included creative Hollywood types like the writer David Mamet and the actor Dustin Hoffman. She felt at home in this trendy, left-handed, vegetarian, "spiritual" kind of Synagogue, and had spent the last couple of years enjoying the community and getting used to this new way of life. This particular Shabbat morning, the Rabbi had gotten up to give his address to the congregation with a very grave look on his face.

"My friends...I'm so sorry to bring you such distressing news." He looked down, took a deep breath and then looked up again. "I was checking my email this morning, and the space shuttle Columbia crashed last night, killing all the astronauts." The congregation gave an audible gasp. "Our hearts go out to our brothers and sisters in Israel as we remember Ilan Ramon, a hero of Eretz Yisrael." Disbelief and sadness washed over the sanctuary. Deborah was stunned as the news sank in. She had never been interested in space travel and didn't know Israel even had astronauts, let alone one on that flight. It suddenly occurred to her that she didn't know very much about modern Israel at all.

After the service, she was talking with some friends about the sad news when one of them mentioned that her client, an elderly lady, was looking for a companion to accompany her for an all expenses paid trip to Israel.

"She fell and broke her hip last year, so she needs someone to be with her. I'd go, only I can't take off from work again."

"How long is it for?" inquired Deborah just a little bit curious.

"It's a guided tour of the whole country, which as you know is only about the size of New Jersey, so ten days I think. Are you interested?"

"Maybe, I'd have to think about it."

"What's to think about? Five-star hotels, guided tours in an air-conditioned bus, did I mention it was free?!"

Deborah laughed, it seemed too good to be true.

Before she knew it, she was meeting the lady and working out the dates. Marilyn was entirely mobile and capable of getting around by herself with a cane, so Deborah wondered why she needed to be accompanied. Maybe it was an insurance thing? She couldn't quite work it out, but anyway it appeared to be a good deal. How did this keep happening to her life? There was some kind of synchronicity thing happening, her life kept unfolding like chapters of a book and all she had to do was keep putting one foot in front of the other. Within a few weeks, she was looking down out of an airplane window at the Mediterranean Sea, and then slowly, through the darkness, the lights of Tel Aviv came into view as they prepared to descend into Ben Gurion airport.

21
Jerusalem

2004

Deborah's first experience of Israel was the King David Hotel. She read in the pamphlet by her bed that it was a five-star, historic 1930s building that had been partly blown up during the Israeli War of Independence by the Palmach resistance fighters. Trust the British to have a five-star hotel as their HQ, thought Deborah. Tea and cake anyone? Kings, Queens, and Presidents had stayed there over the years, and after the incredible and endless breakfast buffet of every kind of cheese, pastry, egg dish, and fresh fruit you could think of, which looked more like art than a buffet, she could see why. When Deborah had first met Marilyn, she had thought maybe she had Alzheimer's or something, but she soon began to realise that Marilyn was really just a sad, lonely old lady. After spending a short time with her, she discerned that she wasn't actually as old and sick as she seemed. She just didn't stop talking! Not ever! It was more like muttering, and it was relentless. Even on the plane, when Deborah had her headphones on, Marilyn was still muttering! They were sharing a room, and that morning when she woke up, Marilyn was already in the middle of a story. Deborah did her best to listen and be patient, she was being paid to keep her company, after all, but she soon worked out that Marilyn was repeating and repeating the same story over and over again. Slowly she put the pieces together and realised it was a story from thirty years ago! Marilyn's husband had divorced her, and the new wife had got the big house in Beverly Hills. That was the only thing she could talk about, for the last thirty years?! Hanging onto this resentment had aged her prematurely and turned her into a lonely, wizened old woman. No wonder she had to pay someone to be a companion, and after a few hours of this Deborah was ready to scream!

After breakfast, they had been directed to meet their tour guide in the beautiful Art Deco lobby of the hotel. Deborah was so happy that it wasn't just another cookie-cutter hotel chain. In her movie travels, she had sometimes woken up and wondered where she was, as one modern hotel room can look like another with no clue if you are in Singapore or Amsterdam. The King David was full of history, and the view of the Old City of Jerusalem from the terrace was magical. It was a small tour group consisting of twelve people, most of whom seemed to be retired doctors and lawyers from the East Coast, and it didn't take them long to get fed up with Marilyn. One retired law professor asked Deborah to please keep a tight rein on Marilyn, and they hadn't even gone anywhere yet! Deborah was tempted to ask him if he wanted her to put on a muzzle on Marilyn but decided to play nice and just smiled. The first stop was, of course, the Western Wall, or The Kotel, as she learned it's called by the locals.

"The Kotel is just a very small part of the original wall that surrounded the first Temple, built in 10th Century BCE by King Solomon," announced Marty their tour guide, as she directed them through the crowds. Marty was probably in her late fifties, a Canadian from Vancouver, and had been living in Israel for almost thirty years. She knew her stuff and had that ease and grace that enabled her to get on with everyone. She was always dressed in shades of purple and carried a parasol high in the air so everyone could follow her through the crowds. Deborah sat down in the Kotel Plaza soaking up the scene. She watched as people from all over the world came to pray as if they were drawn to this spot. They were from all walks of life, religions, and ethnic backgrounds. African women in glorious brightly coloured dresses and turbans, Japanese tourists, Israeli soldiers, and children running in all directions as their mothers prayed and tourists slipped notes into the ancient cracks in the wall - all kinds of people, all together. Some were in deep contemplation, some taking pictures, everyone was welcome, and she could feel that same calm feeling deep inside that she had felt in her bedroom in London. Follow the feeling, Shelly had told her, and so she closed her eyes and whispered some words of gratitude.

As the day went on, she became intrigued by Marty the tour guide. She was really good at her job, but there was something else about her. She had a sneaky sense of humour and just seemed to be at ease with everything, even when one of the group members got lost. She had wandered off into the Armenian Quarter because she wanted to take pictures, and then needed to go to the ER because of a twisted ankle. Marty didn't freak out and was able to keep the other people in the group entertained and calm.

"How do you do that?" asked Deborah later while the others were getting ice cream and drinks at a cafe in the Shuk.

"Do what?" replied Marty surprised.

"Stay so... I think the word is insouciant, calm, nonchalant? I mean you don't seem to be annoyed by their behavior?"

"Hahaha!" laughed Marty. "Well, for one thing,

I'm used to it. I have been doing this so long that I kind of expect there to be at least one idiot who goes off in the wrong direction. I once had a group of retired History Professors who argued with me about every fact I gave, complained about every hotel and every meal, and then two of them had heart attacks!! I earned my money on that trip!"

"Expectations," pondered Deborah. "Yep, that's what trips most of us up. I volunteer as a counsellor, and I see that all the time."

"What kind of counsellor are you, Dvora?"

"Who's Dvora? My name is Deborah! I've been called Debs sometimes but never Dvora!"

"Well it's your Hebrew name, and here you are in Israel, my dear!" Marty continued with a cheeky smile. "Dvora was a prophetess, a leader of her people, a warrior, wise and full of courage."

"Okay," continued Deborah, not sure what to make of her comments. "Well, I volunteer at a kind of "drop-in" advice center in Los Angeles, you know, community center kind of thing. We get all sorts of people, but I was trained in London at a Women's Crisis Center."

"Wow, that's great. I wish I had met you last week!" responded Marty. "I'm a Trauma Counsellor when I'm not Guiding, and we had a workshop that I think you would have liked."

"Really, what kind of workshop?"

"Well, it's called the Three Principles."

"What's that?"

"Well, it's..." Marty paused and took a sip of her herbal tea, "um..." She stopped again to search for words.

"Must have been quite a workshop!" laughed Deborah, amused that Marty couldn't explain it.

"Well, let's see. Back in the Seventies when I was at university in Vancouver, I heard this amazing man called Sydney Banks talk about these ideas...it's not your usual way of understanding something...it's hard to explain..." Marty trailed off, searching for the right words. It was hilarious to Deborah to see this very articulate woman, who had done nothing but talk for the last three hours straight, now struggling with what to say.

"Okay, let me ask you some questions and see if that helps?" offered Deborah, still amused. "Was it about how to treat trauma or...crisis management?"

"No!" cried Marty emphatically.

"Okay, was it about...I don't know, is it a philosophy?"

"No, well, not really."

"Is it a self-help technique thing like CBT or NLP or... the Enneagram?"

"No, it's definitely not a technique."

"Is it a diet? A meditation? A new dance exercise craze done under water!? Come on, give me some kind of clue!"

"Okay," laughed Marty, "I'll try. But whatever I say, it probably isn't." Deborah was intrigued, and grateful that the other members of the group were kept happy by the entertaining and colourful scenes around them. "So, the Three Principles are an understanding of how we all experience life. We all experience life through Thought. You have to be Conscious to do that, and Mind, the source of everything makes all that possible. Our true nature is to be happy and resilient, and Mind, Thought, and Consciousness are the three ways we experience that," Marty sat back in her chair as if she had just finished writing a great novel or given birth to a new century.

Deborah took it in for a moment.

"Okay, so how is that different from any of those other ideas, you know Mindfulness, EFT, and all the hundreds of other therapies out there these days?"

"Well, because it's not a technique or a therapy, it's an *understanding*," explained Marty, "The best thing I can say is that The Principles are descriptive, not prescriptive. Unlike those other therapies that want you to analyse, or reframe your thinking, they all focus on the content of your thoughts so you can work on changing them. The Three Principles point to the fact that you think."

This is like what Sheldon talks about, thought Deborah excitedly. It's not what you are thinking, the Three Principles point you to understand *that* you think. OK.

Marty called the waiter over for the bill and then wrote a name and three words on the back of a napkin and pushed it across the table.

Sydney Banks

Thought

Mind

Consciousness

It had been a long day full of sightseeing and new ideas. Back in her hotel room, Deborah relaxed before getting ready for bed and sat looking out the window. Down below, she could see the terrace where hotel guests sat sipping coffee and brandy under twinkling lights. Across a park on the next hill, she could see the illuminated ancient walls of the Old City. The moon was out, the night sky was clear, and her feelings of gratitude were deeper than ever. She was so excited by what Marty had shared with her, maybe that was why she was here in this magical place? And who was this guy, Sydney Banks? Why hadn't she heard of him before? She had read every self-help book out there, why hadn't she come across any of this before now?

Marilyn was muttering herself to sleep as Deborah went over her conversation with Marty. *Descriptive, not prescriptive*, thought Deborah, *what does that even mean?* She tried to think it through. She remembered what Sheldon had told her about the psychiatrist at the V.A. He had said that *it didn't matter what we thought about what had happened to us; far more important was that we understood that we were the ones doing the thinking.* Aha, maybe that's why he taught them that there is actually nothing to do? If the Principles are a description of how human experience works, then understanding that could lead to...peace of mind? I get it! There's nothing to do because there is nothing wrong, it's just thought passing through, and it's understanding this that sets you free! So other therapies, they are a prescription, a technique for what to do about your thinking, and that's such a misunderstanding! They are just putting more energy into the content of those thoughts and keeping them alive longer! *I knew it!* thought Deborah as she looked around excitedly, but Marilyn had fallen asleep. She wouldn't have understood anyway, thought Deborah, and turned back to look out across the wonderful night laid out in front of her.

The next morning she waited with muttering Marilyn and the others in the lobby of the King David as one of the group went back up to their room to get something. Deborah was excited to see Marty and talk some more. As soon as Marty arrived, she pulled a book out of her bag.

"Here, read this. I need it back before you leave next week, but I think it will answer what I tried to explain yesterday." She handed Deborah a well-loved, slim, paperback book, *The Missing Link*. "It's very easy to read and written by Sydney Banks, the guy who started this whole thing off back in the Seventies after an enlightenment experience. When I first heard him speak back in Vancouver, he blew my mind. We were all into consciousness raising and awareness groups, but this was different. Syd had seen something different, something real and beautiful. Read, and we'll talk some more." Deborah was so excited, she had so many questions. She would have been happy to skip all the archaeological sites they were off to see that day and just stay in the hotel and read, but she resigned herself to her duty to keep an eye on Marilyn instead.

"Thanks!" exclaimed Deborah excitedly as they all got onto a bus to Caesarea and the central coast.

At lunchtime, they sat in the shade of the massive Roman Aqueduct that still stands defiantly on the beach overlooking the Mediterranean Sea. She picked up *The Missing Link* at a random page and read: *"Thought is not reality, yet it is through Thought that our realities are created."*[1] Deborah smiled to herself and read some more.

> If your thoughts wander onto a negative and rocky path, don't take them too seriously. Refrain from analysing, because I guarantee you, you will analyse yourself forever, never reaching an end, and fail bitterly to find peace of mind. What happened in the past may have influenced our present day personal and social problems, but please believe me there is no answer to those problems in the past.[2]

Hmm, thought Deborah, that's it! Her heart jumped as she felt all the dots joining up in her head. She turned to another random page. "*If you live in the past, you can never find happiness. You are trying to live in a reality that no longer exists.*"[3] Deborah almost dropped the book. The words rang so true and strangely familiar, how had she never heard of this guy before? She got up to find Marty.

Marty was off with part of the group who had gone down to the water's edge to dip their toes in the warm Mediterranean Sea.

"Marty! I only read three things, and I love this guy!"

"There, I knew you would like it," Marty grinned as she looked out across the sparkling waves. "We were all hippies back then, searching for enlightenment. My friends and I used to hitchhike around the islands off Vancouver to hear him speak. We were Syd groupies. He blew our minds with his beautiful new ideas. My professors on my doctoral program thought it was all nuts. Keep reading!"

Next, they traveled North to Tiveria for dinner at a restaurant on the pier overlooking the Kinneret. There was a warm breeze, and the moonlight made it seem magical.

"That's Jordan over there," informed Marty, pointing to the other side of the massive lake. "So, will you come back?"

"Me? Uh, yes, I think I will someday," reflected Deborah, finding herself drawn by something she didn't understand.

"If you like the book, there are more. Syd has been teaching something very new. He must be getting on by now, but it was always his wish for this to get out there to help as many people as possible. He shared with us something beyond just learning how the mind works, beyond self-improvement. He was pointing us to a new experience of being, of understanding that these are Spiritual Principles. He showed us how 'Mind' with a capital M, which was his way of saying the Divine, the Loving Source of everything, what you and I might call God, is within us and with us all the time. He could see it - see it in all of us, you, me, everyone - that we are all part of that Source, and once you see this as a spiritual principle, there is no need to be afraid. I was so moved that I came here to Israel to delve deeper into my own rich heritage. People are drawn here by the deep spiritual connection."

"Yes, I kind of see that. Well...ok, I have a few more questions."

"Sure, fire away, but don't get too hung up on the words. The words are just there to help us start the conversation."

"Ok, I get 'Thought' - I mean, I have known for a long time that we are not our thoughts. And I think I get 'Consciousness.' It's awareness, right?"

"Yes. I knew that would make sense to you, our minds are far better at fooling themselves than anything you or your Steven *Schpielberg* will ever come up with! Movies are all about illusion, and your whole reality is created by the Principle of Consciousness at work on your thoughts. The special effects of Consciousness mesmerize us into believing things are real. It uses our five senses, and even physical things like your heart speeding up, to convince us to take certain thoughts seriously."

Deborah thought back over her career... there was that time the studio bigwig thought her tiger was real, and in Australia how the real dogs weren't fooled by her puppet but Jamie the actor was.

"This place is a great example," said Marty. "This restaurant is bustling and crowded. From one person's perspective, it's a really great place to eat: the excellent food, the view of Jordan across the water, the twinkling lights and live music, it's just fabulous. But from another person's perspective, it's crowded, loud, confusing, and even scary to be out over the water like this. The restaurant is the same place, but for different people, the special effects are quite different. That's Consciousness. We all experience things differently depending on our level of Consciousness."

"Ok, I get that, but 'Mind,' this Principle of Mind sounds very... Hippyish or kinda Buddhist to me."

Marty smiled. "Huh, that never occurred to me before...mind you, it was the Seventies! Syd was way ahead of his time. His ideas have been spreading slowly for many years now, but sometimes I worry they will get watered down. I mean Self-Help has become big business, and I wonder if the Principles will become packaged up into just another self-help technique. Seeing that it's your thoughts is just the opening of the door to this understanding. Seeing that they are Spiritual Principles, the spiritual nature of everything is something else, something deeper. It's not something you can teach or sell. It has to come from an insight, a sight from within." Marty took a sip of her wine. "But like this, there is a Source of everything. Look around you, everything you see is made up of thought, and Mind is the source of all those thoughts."

"Ok, now you've lost me!"

"See, when you said, 'I get Thought,' you meant thinking, right? Well, thinking is only one thing you can do with the gift of Thought!" Deborah raised her eyebrows as if to say *what?*! "I know, it freaked me out a bit too when I first heard that. I panicked, maybe there was something I was missing out on, some Kabbalah thing that I didn't know about!" said Marty as she waved her hands in the direction of the mystical town of Tzfat up in the mountains they would be visiting the next day. "But there is...daydreaming, there is anxiety. There is creating...imagination, insecurity...there are lots of things you can do with the raw material of Thought. It's kind of like paint. You can paint a portrait, repaint your house, or paint your nails. It's the same stuff being used in different ways, and you can choose what to do with it."

Deborah suddenly remembered driving in LA. "One time I put the radio on in my car to NPR and they were in the middle of an interview with some artist, and the interviewer was asking, 'So you can picture your whole design in your head without needing to draw it first?' with such incredulity and I thought, can't everyone do that?"

Marty laughed, "No, we can't! Well, actually we can, but not to the degree you obviously do! I mean I can create dinner for my family in my head, but I couldn't create how to make a talking tiger or a wedding dress like you can without drawing it first, and then I wouldn't know where to start. You do all that in your head using creative thought!"

"OK, but how is Mind the source of that?"

"Where do your ideas come from, Dvora?" Marty listened intently for the answer.

"I don't know...out of the blue, I guess?"

"Ok, well the 'blue' is just another way to say Mind or God, and It gives us the gift of Thought. What we do with it is up to us. Mind is the Spiritual Source, the Intelligence of everything that guides us through life, and Thought is the spiritual energy, the raw material that you are given to turn that guidance into experience via the special effects of Consciousness."

"And what about the subconscious, how does that fit into all of this?"

Marty laughed, "OK. First, let's differentiate between the subconscious and the unconscious. People seem to interchange them, but this is how I understand it, and I'm no expert. The unconscious is that part of your brain that takes care of things like breathing, heartbeat, and digestion. I think doctors call it autonomic, you don't have to think about it, behaviours and bodily functions that just happen, right? Although there is research now to show we can influence it. But the subconscious is just a concept made up by psychiatry, like a bogeyman to make everyone feel like they have to analyse the past and if they don't, the bogeyman is going to get them! If you think about it, what most people refer to as their subconscious is just fearful thinking."

"And so it doesn't need dealing with in any special way, it's just more thinking?"

"Exactly. Once you get that it's all just spooky, spiritual energy going through the mind and that Divine Mind is there to love and guide you all the time, then the fears start to fall away. There is no psychological subconscious monster under the bed who is out to get you, that's just thought masquerading as a concept, and concepts are all made of thought."

"Wow! Then the idea that your subconscious can manipulate you or that your behaviour is determined by your subconscious is...it's just more anxious thinking...just like my *Myth of Low Self-Esteem*, it's just thinking going up and down! I knew it!!" cried Deborah excitedly.

"Yes, Syd taught us that as soon as you stop taking those thoughts seriously, they lose their power over you; you don't even have to do anything about them, they will fade away, and you will see your innate well-being. A Well of Being if you like. It's like we are innocent, only our thoughts want to hold us and others guilty!" Deborah was so intrigued. "The Psychiatric profession wants us to believe we are damaged, guilty, or bad somehow, but we, everyone, every single human being is innocent; we just get sucked in by some stinky thinking sometimes, that's all!

Underneath that stressful thinking, your mind, everyone's mind, is perfectly healthy. I can sit here and enjoy the moment, or I can start worrying if the bus driver will be outside to pick us up in five minutes. Which reminds me, "Hey guys, let's get this show on the road, time to go!"

When Deborah got back to the hotel, she couldn't wait to check her email in the guest computer room and tell everyone about Sydney Banks. There was an email from Anton, who was still surfing, one from Bob asking when she would be back, and one from Kristi, who was excited to say she was setting up her own Executive Personal Assistant Agency. Abby and Carol just wanted to say hi, and there was one from Shelly with lots of exclamation marks in the subject line: "**You won't believe this!!!!**"

Deborah was intrigued and quickly opened the email.

> Remember Angela from about 15 years ago, I think she was one of your first clients here in London? The one who prosecuted her stepfather?

Deborah cast her mind back... Oh yeah, Angela was the one she went to Shoreditch police station with.

> Well, she faked it!!

What?!! thought Deborah.

She made it all up! wrote Shelly.

Deborah sat up straight, she couldn't believe it!

> She just came to see me and told me the whole story. She hated him because he had refused her advances and so she punished him by telling lies that he had touched her! Can you believe it?!!

NO, I CAN'T!! cried Deborah out loud, still in disbelief.

> She has confessed and came to tell me. Her stepfather was jailed for 2 years and refuses to talk to her, and her mum is beside herself with grief all over again. She's grown up now and knows she was wrong and wanted me to tell you how sorry she was for dragging you into it.

Deborah went up to her room and sat back on her bed. Wow. She remembered Francesca warning them that this kind of thing could happen but...but, wow! She thought about Angela, and many of their conversations came flooding back. Angela had often talked about her low self-esteem and how her stepfather had damaged it, and that's why she needed to report him to get back her self-worth. Deborah laughed to herself, Angela's self-esteem was very well intact if she was making passes at her mother's new husband...and the chutzpah of going through with all that drama, the prosecution, Oh My! She could only have thought it was ok to punish him if she thought she deserved better from him? No low self-esteem there! It confirmed for Deborah that what most people meant by low self-esteem was actually just low thinking, to use Syd's words. It was Angela's thinking and her levels of consciousness that had gone up and down, not her true nature, that pure something, that internal, special spark, that...that part of us that can never change be damaged or need improving. Angela clearly had some contaminated thinking and had made some very, very bad decisions, but her pure, holy self was there all the time. Somehow, now that she was older, she was able to find her way back to the wisdom that had always been there. Wow.

It was hard to fall asleep, what with the news from Shelly and the conversation with Marty... Deborah's mind was spinning. She went back to the conversation that she had had with Shelly about the Wizard of Oz. As she lay there, it occurred to her that "somewhere over the rainbow" was really just a thought too, it's not an actual place... *mm, of course it's not an actual place*, thought Deborah, as she mused her sleepy way through this idea. But 'somewhere' is just a concept, that somewhere place, over there, where everything will be better is just a thought, and if concepts are made up of thoughts...all our suffering is only ever happening in our minds... *Syd was right!*

Angela's misunderstanding was that she thought her problem was that her stepfather refusing her advances was the cause of her suffering, and that led her to believe she needed to punish him in order to make herself feel better. That was a belief that she had created and her consciousness had added in the special effects to make it seem real... She had created a reality that her 'over the rainbow' place would be when her stepfather was hurting like she was?

Deborah was beginning to fall asleep...and...boy...what a mess! Dorothy and Angela...all of us, we are actually only ever experiencing our thoughts about reality, not the reality itself... The thoughts, the pot of gold, is on the inside. What did Marty say, wellbeing, a Well of Being... Somewhere over the rainbow is really...right here...right now...

22
Tzfat

2004

As they drove out of Tiveria the next afternoon to head up to Tzfat, Deborah was lost in thought. It was like everything she had ever wondered about how the mind works was falling into place. She was loving the book. It was as if these Principles that Marty had told her about had given her a vocabulary to articulate something she always knew deep inside. As she gazed out of the window of their tour bus, she was fascinated by how the landscape had changed so much in such a small country, from barren deserts in the South to lush, green plains, to the snowy mountains further North. It was actually very similar to California on a smaller scale, with only the occasional camel or boy herding goats to give it away. Everyone was excited to visit the ancient city of Tzfat and soak up its mystical history. High up in the mountains, surrounded by forests and stunning views, its windy, cobbled streets had been home to Kabbalistic writers and poets in the 1500s. Now it was the "spirituality" and Artists' Colony, which attracted tourists on the lookout for some unique artifact to take home. They drove higher and higher around hair-pin bends through the forests, pine trees on both sides. She continued to daydream about the new ideas, as Marilyn muttered away in the seat behind her and Marty gave them information about their surroundings and destination. It amused her to think that Shakespeare was writing at the same time that Tzfat was experiencing its mystical heyday, and then she remembered that she had recently learned that Martin Luther King was born the same year as Anne Frank. *Curious*, she thought, *time is such a curious thing*.

The bus let them off around the corner of the old, but elegant boutique hotel they would be staying in for the next two nights, as it couldn't quite fit in the narrow street. The driver promised to deliver the bags by hand himself, so they followed Marty in through the front doors. The group was invited out onto a beautiful veranda that overlooked the Upper Galilee Valley, and they sat to watch the sunset spread glorious orange and lavender light across the evening sky.

"Tomorrow morning we will tour the city, and then in the afternoon you will have free time to explore the Artist Colony," announced Marty.

"Can we talk some more in the afternoon?" Deborah asked Marty after she had finished talking to the group.

"Sure, but don't you want to discover some art?"

"What? Nah, that's for tourists and Marilyn couldn't care less."

"Ok, I know a lovely cafe where we can relax, and Marilyn can watch the passersby," proposed Marty with a wink as she started to motion to the group that she was saying good night.

"Great, thanks! Good night!" Deborah turned to collect Marilyn and so they could go find their room.

"Where's Marilyn?" asked Deborah whipping around trying to see where she was. No one responded.

"Anyone seen Marilyn?!" yelled Deborah, but everyone shrugged as if to say, not my problem.

"Maybe she went to the bathroom?" suggested one of the group members.

Oh no! thought Deborah and darted back inside. She found the bathrooms just off the dining room, but no one was there.

"Have you seen an elderly lady come through here?" she asked the receptionist.

"An American?"

"Yes!"

"No."

"Please call Marty Fox's room and tell her to come to the lobby. Tell her, tell her I've lost Marilyn!"

Deborah started to rush through the old hotel looking in every corner and alcove, but Marilyn wasn't anywhere. She went back out the front door and looked up and down the tiny street. She couldn't see far, as it twisted around a corner, but there was no Marilyn.

"What happened?" cried Marty running out behind her.

"I don't know! One minute she was there and the next, she was gone!"

"Ok, I'll call the police, and you start looking around the streets."

"But I don't know Tzfat!"

"Well, neither does Marilyn! Would you rather talk to the police?"

Deborah ran down the street. There were little, old houses and shops and alleys in all directions. None of the streets were wide enough for a car, and they all either went uphill or down. Deborah couldn't imagine that Marilyn had gotten very far with her limp and cane, but where was she? She looked in every shop and cafe and finally decided to go back to the hotel to see if she had shown up. As she turned to go back for a second, it occurred to her she didn't know the name of the hotel or the street she had come from! All she knew was that it was at the top of a hill! She took a deep breath and traced her steps backward, trying to remember which way she had come. Finally, after a few false turns, she turned into the tiny street of their hotel and saw the flashing lights of a police car. She ran in, not knowing what to expect.

In the lobby sat Marty comforting Marilyn, while a young female police officer and the bus driver were yelling at each other.

"Where were you, Marilyn?" cried Deborah, catching her breath.

"Nobody cares, nobody listens to me, nobody," muttered Marilyn.

"She didn't get off the bus when we arrived!" explained Marty, "so when the driver went to park up around the corner he didn't realise there was anyone left on the bus and locked her in while he went back and forth with the bags, poor thing." She handed Marilyn a glass of water.

"Oh no! I'm so sorry!" apologized Deborah. "Are you ok?"

"No one cares he gave my house to that witch, *my* house! No one cares what happens to me."

"She's fine," observed Marty with half a smile.

The policewoman and the driver were still yelling at each other in Hebrew, and now the receptionist and the manager had joined in, so the three ladies left them to it and went to their rooms.

When Deborah woke up the next morning, she had never been so happy to see Marilyn. They got dressed and went down to join the others for breakfast.

"I don't know how you put up with it," commented one of the tour group. "She's impossible."

Deborah just smiled and got herself some eggs and orange juice.

It was a lovely morning. They strolled through the

ancient city following Marty in her flowing purple, up stone steps and down enchanting cobbled streets and alleys, visiting ancient synagogues and looking out over splendid views of the valley. All of the window frames, doors, shutters, and gates were painted with different shades of aquamarine blue. Ranging from almost turquoise to royal blue, it was enchanting against the antiquated stone. Even the plastic chairs were blue. Marty told them that the famous 16th Century Rabbi Yosef Karo had said that blue reminds us of heaven, and heaven reminds us to pray, and then she told them that it also repels mosquitoes apparently so either way, it was delightful.

The group was set free to have lunch wherever they wanted and to explore on their own for the afternoon. Deborah and Marilyn followed Marty to a small cafe in a courtyard looking down over the main street. There were tables and chairs under the shade of a beautiful old vine. It dripped from a gnarled ancient olive tree that looked so old, it could have been planted by Noah after the flood.

"Shalom, Marty!" greeted the owner warmly and welcomed them to their seats.

Marty gave a huge smile. "Shalom, Mosheleh!" They chatted in Hebrew for a few minutes and then Marty sat down.

"An old friend?" wondered Deborah.

Marty laughed, "He's my cousin's nephew. He grew up in Brooklyn but he's been here a while, he's a good boy. I ordered lunch for us all. Moshe will bring us a taste of everything, his hummus is the best in Tzfat."

"Ok, great!" Deborah was unable to wait any longer with her questions. "Marty, I can see this understanding helping someone who has PTSD or, say, a mild depression, but what about something like schizophrenia? This can't work for serious things like mental diseases, can it?" Marty sat back in her chair and smiled.

"Syd taught us that all mental illness is just people listening to their own low thinking and believing it to be true... I want to ask you something," Marty continued cautiously. "Last night you said something like, *One minute she was there and the next minute she was gone*? But our friend here never left the bus... Do you see how your consciousness played a trick on you? You imagined she was with you, but she wasn't."

"Ugh, I know. I couldn't stop thinking about that last night, I feel terrible. I was so lost in my thoughts that I wasn't present." Then something clicked in Deborah's mind... "I get it! I was about to call it daydreaming, but I was experiencing a reality that was created by my thoughts, not what was actually happening around me!"

"Exactly. You and I call that daydreaming, but take it a bit further, and doctors call it delusions and hallucinations, and then they call it mental illness!! It usually starts small, like worrying about what someone might have said about you at work, and then someone doesn't laugh at your joke. Soon the insecure thoughts are so distracting that you are afraid to go into the office, and then you lose your job. The thoughts get worse, and you listen and repeat them over and over. Soon your world has shrunk, and you can't see a way out, and all you can hear are the voices in your head that are driving you crazy!"

"Yes! that's exactly what happened to me, but I'm talking about actual mental disease?"

"OK, so there are brain diseases like Dementia and brain tumours for sure, but you're talking about what's in the DSM books, right?" Deborah nodded. "Well, when I was in University, we were taught that it was a list of mental illnesses, but what I know now is that it is really a list of the way people cope with the kind of stressful thoughts I just described."

"What do you mean?" asked Deborah as Moshe and another waiter brought out an array of the most delicious looking salads and hummus. Matbucha, grilled eggplant with tahina, olives, cheeses, and freshly baked pita that was still warm and puffed up filled their table.

"Ooh, yum!"

"Thank you, my darling boy, it looks delightful!" complimented Marty. Moshe placed a beautiful handmade artisan blue plate in front of each of them and encouraged them to start...

"Well, could you see that some people cope with that kind of distressed thinking by overeating? Some might cope by drinking or violence or isolating, talking to themselves for comfort? Others cope by relying on rituals like washing their hands over and over, or cutting themselves, some by relying on drugs, which could be from a doctor or a dealer. The number of "illnesses" in the DSM increases every time they put out a new edition! You'd have to ask yourself, are there really that many new illnesses, or are they just new ways to cope with distressing thoughts? You should talk to my nephew Isaac when you get back to the States, he has done a lot of research into this. Call me cynical, but it seems to me that they are systematically medicalising every natural human experience so they can sell more drugs, but that's another conversation!"

"But...but that changes everything! If people could understand that they don't have to take those thoughts seriously, that they will just pass by like...like those buses down there, then they wouldn't get sick, they wouldn't get so far down the road that they need medication to shut the noise up!"

"Exactly! There is no way to stop thoughts, they just keep coming no matter how enlightened you are. It's natural to have thought, it's the way we are made.

There will always be another thought, another bus, and when you see that you are free to choose whether or not to get on that bus, space starts to appear between the thoughts."

Deborah interrupted, "And that's where peace of mind comes in! It's the way the system was created!"

"Yes!"

The three ladies finished the delicious lunch, then Moshe brought out coffee for Marty and two tall glass mugs of foaming hot chocolate for Deborah and Marilyn.

"There's no chocolate in this, it's just milk!" snapped Marilyn.

"It's the way they do it here, my darling," laughed Marty, "Look, it's got chunks of real chocolate at the bottom, you just have to stir it."

"I've always had this idea," continued Deborah, "that when people say they have low self-esteem it's really just the quality of their thinking that is going up and down. In fact, it's usually a resentment that people or life isn't treating them right. If they really had low self-esteem they would be surprised at being treated well. It's usually just an excuse to blame and complain that the world isn't treating them the way they think they deserve!"

"Sure but it's an innocent mistake. Everyone is inherently healthy, full of wisdom and grace. It just hides under that distressed thinking sometimes. We all make up stories in our heads about how we think things should be and when that story goes wrong some of us can get very ill. But there is good news. I have seen many times, people who were diagnosed with serious mental illnesses, who have been in and out of hospitals for years, get well with this understanding."

"Most people think I'm crazy," announced Marilyn all of a sudden. "I could tell you a thing or two about distress, but at least it gets their attention...sometimes," and then she went back to spooning up her hot chocolate.

Deborah and Marty looked at Marilyn curiously, then at each other. "I've tried," sighed Deborah, sitting back in her chair with a slight wink. "But until we are ready to let go, there's not much anyone can do. I know I wasn't ready until I was."

23
Tel Aviv

2004

The last two days of the trip were spent in Tel Aviv, visiting the Diaspora Museum and the beaches. Tel Aviv was not a pretty city, much of its older architecture dated from before the founding of the State and reminded Deborah of the tenements she had seen crumbling in Eastern Europe, along with the Soviet Union from which many of these first modern Israeli settlers had fled. The rest of it was brand new, with skyscrapers and bustling shopping malls. The younger generation had turned it into the New York of the Middle East, always open and always busy. It had an entirely different feel from that of Jerusalem: the pace, the people, the atmosphere. That night they had a traditional style Friday night meal in the hotel, and one of the older men fumbled his way through the Kiddush blessing over the wine before they all sat down to eat. Deborah soaked it all in, the last ten days had been eye-opening in so many ways.

After dinner, she walked with Marty along the Tel Aviv beachfront in front of their hotel. Marilyn had gone to bed, so they strolled leisurely in the night air.

"So what about, say, for example, when someone says they get anxiety out of nowhere, how would you explain that?" Deborah wanted to understand as much as she could before the end of the trip.

"Oh gosh, I'm sure my psychology professors

would disagree, but I would say there was probably some thought first. When people get honest, they see that their panic attacks are always preceded by anxious thoughts, but ok, I'll try. So I would say maybe they just weren't aware of it. Thought is like an iceberg, you know, most of it is submerged under the water."

"But a few days ago you said that there is no such thing as the subconscious, you can't have it both ways! You can't say there is submerged thought and dismiss the concept of subconscious thought!!" challenged Deborah, eagerly.

Marty stopped and turned to Deborah, she had a puzzled look on her face like she was working up to giving birth to another speech. She paused and then said carefully, "It could seem like two labels for the same thing, but I just got it." She hopped from one foot to another in excitement. "Do I, Marty, have submerged thoughts? Of course I do, we all do! We all have so much thinking we are not aware of. But as I consider that I have submerged thought, there's no fear there; it doesn't scare me! Why? Because they're not in my consciousness until I think them, therefore they can't hurt or scare me. The concept of the subconscious is all wrapped up in fearful thinking, the concept itself promotes a fear that something is lurking out there in the dark, don't you see?!" She pointed out to the dark horizon across the Mediterranean Sea. "It's the concept that is causing the distress, not the submerged thoughts, the concept that the bogeyman subconscious is going to get you if you're not on guard. That's what is producing the fear, not the submerged unthought thoughts, do you see the difference?"

"I think so," admitted Deborah slowly. "But what about people who say that trauma is held in the body like back pain?"

"As I said, my psychology professors would not

agree and I'm not a medical doctor, but the way I understand it is that any unresolved thoughts, like resentment, activates our stress response, and that allostatic load is like a load of bricks, a burden, it weighs us down and hurts the body until it is dealt with. That's why I find this understanding so helpful with clients who are suffering from the results of unresolved thought. They are having a physical experience of the innocent misunderstanding of thought, not the made up demon of subconscious." Marty put her hands up like claws and made a monster coming to get you kind of face. They laughed and started to walk back to the hotel.

Deborah told Marty about the email from Shelly and the drama and pain Angela had caused.

"One of my most favourite things I heard Syd say," offered Marty, "is *'If the only thing people learned was not to be afraid of their own experience, that alone would change the world.'* If your client had learned to not be afraid of her experience, she wouldn't have needed to destroy that guy's life and break her mother's heart."

"Quite!" agreed Deborah.

The next morning it was Shabbat, and Deborah found herself walking past the hotel synagogue between the dining room and the lobby. It was an ugly 1970s synagogue, no ornate carvings or ancient inscriptions, just fake wood paneling and some dusty orange and brown macrame wall hangings that should have been cast out of the Promised Land a long time ago. She could see an odd collection of male tourists and aging locals praying, which made it seem ok to go in. She sat self-consciously at the back of the women's section, where there was one other lady, who handed her a tired, old prayer book. It was all in Hebrew, she had no chance of following along, so she just sat and listened. She listened to the singing, the chanting of the Torah reading, she listened to the silence as the men prayed privately, and then again with the Rabbi leading. She didn't understand a word, but she didn't need to. The idea of a Divine Mind, The Source of Everything, was clearly in this room. No words were needed, she understood, and she recognised the Quiet. She fell into the Well of Being like she did that time in her room when Quiet came to save her. *Peace of mind is when thought slows down*, she thought to herself. *It's the space between the thoughts.* She started to see how her idea of ignoring negative thoughts had been just a beginning - beyond the relief of a quiet mind is peace, and the relationship we can all have with that Divine Source of everything, no matter what each person wants to call it. She didn't even have to ignore the thoughts, they would just go on by, by themselves. All she had to do was slow down to the speed of Peace, and there it was, where it is for everyone, waiting, perfect and always available. Deborah saw that she didn't need anything or anyone to make this moment better, she felt peaceful, whole, and present just being.

The peacefulness continued for the rest of the day. She sat with Marilyn as she continued to mutter about her evil ex-husband, and occasionally Deborah read to her from *The Missing Link* for her own enjoyment until it was time for a light supper and bed. She said a quiet thank you to this quiet peacefulness and lay down to sleep, they were leaving for the airport in the morning, the trip was almost over.

Sunday morning down in the lobby, she looked for Marty to say her goodbyes.

"Thank you so much, for everything. The tour, the adventures... these Principles," Deborah handed back the book and gave Marty a special hug. "I really enjoyed them, and yes, I will be buying my own as soon as I get back to LA!"

"I'm so glad! I think you will find they get deeper and deeper the more you understand them. You watch, they will spread and change the world. You have my number and email, please stay in touch and don't forget to look up my nephew Isaac and his wife Becca in New York. Let me know as soon as you are coming back...Dvora!" called Marty with a big smile.

They hugged again, while the rest of the group said their goodbyes and thank yous to Marty and boarded the bus to the airport.

24
Venice Beach

Deborah was half asleep on her sofa in the late afternoon, still recovering from the trip and jet lag, when she vaguely became aware she could hear police or was it ambulance sirens. At first, they seemed far away, but as she became more awake, she realised they had stopped at the back of her house. She sat up, grabbed a sweatshirt, and ran out to see what was happening. Paramedics were going in and out of the back of Sheldon's house. Her heart jumped! She ran to see what had happened, but it was too late. There was a body wrapped in a shroud being carried out on a stretcher as she heard Sheldon scream from the front room.

"Do you know this guy?" inquired one of the paramedics as he met her at the back door.

"Yes, I live right there, what happened?!" Deborah could hardly catch her breath.

"Can you sit with him, I need to get back up."

Deborah went over to Sheldon where he was sitting on the sofa, he was staring down, face white, and his body rigid with terror.

"Sheldon, it's Deborah, I'm here, I'm right here!" She knelt down in front of him. He didn't respond, his eyes were glazed, and he looked far away, so she took his hand, it was clammy and stiff.

"Sheldon, Sheldon." He didn't respond. "Sheldon, can you feel me squeeze your hand?" No reaction. "It's

Deborah, I'm right here with you...if you can hear me, squeeze my hand."

Sheldon squeezed her hand gently.

Deborah had to think fast, she knew she had to get him back to the present moment and for some bizarre reason, she thought about what they did in movies.

"Sheldon, who is the President?"

He looked up slightly, "Some idiot I didn't vote for..." Tears started rolling down his face, and a look of deep anguish filled his eyes.

"What happened?" demanded Deborah.

"She slipped, she slipped in the bath! How could this have happened? Why didn't I come home earlier?! Why didn't we have one of those mats?! Oh my God, what am I going to do without her?!" cried Sheldon as he started to shake uncontrollably. He turned and curled up into a ball. He began to wail, eerie sounds came from deep inside him like a wounded animal.

Deborah gasped in disbelief, she couldn't believe what was happening.

Apparently, Jennifer had been taking a shower in the bathtub, slipped, hit her head and drowned in just a few inches of water! The medic came back with a doctor and a police officer. They were sympathetic, but cautious, asking lots of questions: When did Sheldon get home? When did he last see Jennifer? What state of mind was she in? It all seemed pretty routine, and Sheldon answered as best he could. When they had done what they needed to do and finished asking all their questions, they left him alone. Somehow he pulled it together and then left in a taxi to go stay with close friends, and Deborah went home. As she sat down in her kitchen, she noticed she was shaking and that she was breathing really fast. She called Abby, told her what had happened, and jumped in the car for some TLC.

A few days later a policeman knocked on her door. She took a step backward nervously.

"Just doing some routine inquiries regarding the death at 146, can we come in?"

"Uh, yes, I guess so?" Deborah stepped aside as he came straight past her, followed by a policewoman.

It was a surreal moment to have two LAPD police officers in her living room. She was acutely aware that they had guns. British Bobbies don't have guns. It was the closest she had been to guns apart from seeing all the young off-duty soldiers in Israel with an Uzi machine gun slung over their shoulders, but all she could think was, *there are two police officers in my living room right now armed with guns*!

"We understand you knew the deceased and her husband..." the officer paused to look at his notes, "Mr...Sheldon Wolfe?"

"Yes, you know that?" Deborah wondered where this was going.

"Would you say they had a good relationship?"

"Very good, they adored each other!"

"No problems then that you are aware of? Nothing that would make you...concerned?" inquired the woman officer.

"Not at all, they were like teenagers in love. Why?"

"Thank you, Miss. If you think of anything we should know, please contact us at the Santa Monica police station," said the male officer, and they left.

Deborah was confused, what was all that about?! She was afraid to ask them anything for fear of saying the wrong thing.

As soon as they left, she called Sheldon to see how he was doing.

"I'm so sorry. Did the police bother you?"

"No, it's ok, they were here just now asking

questions. What's going on?"

"They think I killed her!"

"What!!"

"They say that because I pulled the plug out of the bath that I was trying to destroy evidence!! That I had something to hide!! I could never hurt Jennifer, she was my life! What was I supposed to do? Leave her there drowning!!" cried Sheldon.

"That's insane!" cried Deborah. "Don't worry, big guy, this will get sorted out, they are just being stupid, and it will blow over. I'm sending big hugs down the phone, just tell me what I can do to help."

"I'll be home in a few days...just be my friend."

"Of course, anything you want, just ask."

Deborah put the phone down, she couldn't believe it. How was this happening?

A few days after the funeral, Sheldon knocked on her door.

"Hey! Come in. How are you?"

"Ok...considering...I guess." He sighed and sat down in Deborah's armchair. "I'm so tired, I can't sleep and..." He started to cry.

"That's ok, it's normal, you are doing amazing."

"They dropped the investigation. Can you believe they thought I did that?! Did you see the size of the black lump on her beautiful face? Did they really think I could have done that to her?"

"Thank God that's over!" cried Deborah with relief.

"Actually, would you take me to the copyshop, I need to fax the death certificate to some office and I need someone else to drive, I feel a little bit shaky today..."

"Of course, no problem."

Deborah drove Sheldon to the Marina to take care

of the paperwork and helped him get some groceries. She continued to look in on him every day and took him out for a drive up the coast a few times just to get him out the house and to see the ocean.

As the days and weeks went by, she was amazed at how well he was coping. He was very, very sad, he looked and moved as if the wind had been knocked out of him, slowly and carefully, but he kept moving, taking care of things, and putting other people at ease when they visited. He talked about how he had lost his best friend and about all the plans and all the dreams they had for getting old together that meant nothing now, but who could blame him? That was all gone. He talked about feeling lost and alone. He cried openly and, in turn, comforted their friends who were distraught by the tragedy. But even in these dark moments, he seemed to have a resilience that gave him the strength to cope. He talked of gratitude for the time they had together and shared sweet stories about how they met, her brilliant young mind, her favorite music, and how really messy she was when she cooked. Deborah was in awe of his inner strength and how he was still available to the people around him despite his own grief. Many of the grieving people Deborah had worked with were totally consumed with their own pain, but not Sheldon. He would cry and feel deep sadness, and then it would pass, and he was in the moment again.

"How do you do that?" asked Deborah.

"What?"

"I don't know, you just seem to be coping so well. I mean I know you are devastated, how much you loved her and miss her, but somehow your pain isn't...consuming you?"

Sheldon sipped his coffee as they sat on his deck

looking out across the water. "Actually, I feel like my heart has been ripped out of my chest." Then he paused, "but the strange thing is there is a beautiful peace deep inside of me that can't be touched by the grief. I found it after my breakdown .... after 'Nam. The truth is it had always been there, everyone has it, it's always there, like the sun. Even when clouds cover up the sun, it's always there. Jen knew it, she knew it naturally because she was young and full of hope. I had to find it the hard way." He paused for a minute and then said, "I don't know if I would call it God, but I think it's what other people mean when they talk about God, and I find it helps to talk with It.

Deborah didn't quite understand what he meant, but she could feel it. It was like when she sat in the Synagogue in Tel Aviv, the Well of Being.

Sheldon sighed, "Bob Marley said it best: 'You will never know how strong you are until being strong is the only choice you have.'"

Deborah had been hired on another movie, so she dug out the list of books that Marty had given her to take with her on location. She drove over to the Marina to look for them in the bookstore and was surprised to find them so easily, just sitting innocently on the shelf in the self-help/spiritual aisle, as if they had been waiting for her all along. How come she had never seen them in all her searches for help before? She was baffled that it wasn't till now that she had heard of this guy, Sydney Banks.

As soon as she had settled into her hotel room she started to read *The Enlightened Gardener*. It was a sweet book, and she found its descriptions of the English Countryside quaint and nostalgic. It reminded her of childhood holidays and long summers in the West of England, a far ride from the Las Vegas Strip where she was staying now. That evening she called Sheldon to check in and asked if he had ever read either of the books.

"Not sure, I know the Shrink at the V.A. used to read to us, but I don't think those books were out yet... Read me something?"

Deborah opened *The Missing Link* at a random page. "*Thought is not reality, yet it is through thought that reality is created.*"[1] They both paused to take it in.

"I can dig that." Sheldon continued, "I mean, I get really weird thoughts sometimes, really far out thoughts, but I know it's just my mind playing tricks on me, so I don't get weirded out. I know I don't have to act on them, I can let them go by, it's not real."

"What is reality, then?" wondered Deborah curiously.

"Well, that's a good question," Sheldon was starting to come back to his old self. "I'm not sure I know. In those first few hours after I found Jen in the bath, I think I lost all touch with reality, but I guess it was still going on around me."

"It was just a few minutes actually," corrected Deborah.

"What was?"

"When you were gone inside, away with the fairies, as it were."

"Really? It felt like hours, that's weird."

"You know when I was mugged? Well for about ten years after I would describe myself as having an out-of-body experience. It was as if I was suspended about twenty feet up in the air like a cat up a tree, looking down at something I couldn't possibly understand. I could see myself on the ground and the guys beating me. I could hear myself screaming for my life, and it was...not like slow motion exactly, but what must have only been a minute seemed to last about five? In those moments my body didn't contain me, and I felt free, almost fluid and...kind of, I dunno, it's hard to explain. Then about ten years after the attack, I started remembering it differently; that when they were hitting me, I was really deep inside of me, like I was deep inside one of those blow-up beach balls. It was like I was protected by a cushion of...air? I could feel the sensation of my body being knocked around like a tree being pounded by a gale force wind, but they couldn't touch me, the essential me. They couldn't hurt me because I was deep inside...because I'm not fragile, I'm...not my body. But you know what the weird thing is, now I feel...like they are both true. They were both happening at the same time!"

"That's trippy," ventured Sheldon, "it's almost like the body is a metaphor to hold the spirit. When we disconnect from the body, we are fluid, I guess?"

"Yes! It was like I was way up there and deep inside me at the same time! Like time and space didn't apply."

"Time isn't linear for sure, it can feel like it is most of the time, but it speeds up and slows down, and the present is the past as soon as it's happened. I guess if God invented time, He can do whatever He wants with it. I know if I were God, I would mess with everyone's heads!" Sheldon gave a little chuckle. It was nice to hear him lighten up a little.

"I get that. It's spooky, but kind of comforting in a way. Syd says next that it's what we humans put into our thoughts that dictates what we think of life... Back when I thought life was out to get me, at the end, I was frozen to the wall in my apartment, unable to conceive of a life without pain. I couldn't remember a time before the pain, and I 'knew' that for me, there would never be a time without pain," confessed Deborah. "Just like Marianne Williamson says, 'Nervous breakdowns are highly underrated forms of spiritual experience.'"

"Hmm, I think that's true. I think many people are scared to really let go because they fear they won't be able to get back, and yet it's usually the people who are hurting so much that they can't hold on anymore who get to experience real freedom. They let go and find out they can fly."

"That's beautiful, Sheldon."

"See, that's the thing. Everything is made of thought. There are no exceptions. Everything we experience is through thought and made up of thought. I have waves of real, deep sadness, and I have learned that the waves will pass over me and that I can't come to any harm, I will be ok. I think there is a place behind the thinking, a place you can fall into where the silence is, where the sun always shines. It's always there, we just get distracted by things like grief or self-pity. I used to think I had to work hard at making the negative thinking go away to get to that sweet place, but it's always there if I just look in the right direction, if I just look inside."

Deborah smiled. "I think I just realised something. After my third attack, my thinking got very, very dark very quickly. I was about to give up, but I think it was maybe because I was done trying, trying so very hard, that I fell into that place you are talking about. Ever since that time, there has always been the option of that quiet place. Before that time, the only option on offer was to check out."

"That thing, the Space, that quiet space where we find courage and inspiration, the V.A. psychiatrist called that Mind. He said it was the Source of everything. After 'Nam the shrinks that told us to relive and relive all that horror as a way to neutralise the memories - they got it wrong. They were really trying to help, but they kept us stuck in the past, a past that had been gone for years. All it did was either prolong the horror or make us numb. Being in that quiet place is very different from being numb. Numb has a heavy feeling. You'd think you can't feel anything being numb, but you can, you feel, well...heavy, but the quiet place is, well, it's warm and comforting. It's light, alive and fresh, with real possibility of what's possible right now... What does he say about looking at the past for answers?" asked Sheldon.

Deborah thumbed through the book as Sheldon relaxed in his favourite chair back in LA.

"If you live in the past, you can never find happiness. You are trying to live in a reality that no longer exists."

25
New York

Deborah sat in the departure lounge at JFK waiting
for her gate to be announced for her connecting flight
back to LA. She had been to another location for the
movie and was glad to be going home. She was getting
tired of the film business. She loved the traveling,
being paid silly money to be creative and see parts of
the world she would never have got to see otherwise,
but the egos, the delusions, and the drama behind the
scenes were getting to her. On this last movie, the
director had had a massive tantrum on the
soundstage: shouting at the crew, calling names, and
throwing around threats. Deborah had been off to the
side fixing one of the animatronic puppets in a
temporary workshop when she heard shouting and
had come out to see what was happening. What she
saw was the director storm off, cursing and yelling as
he made his way off the stage, and then hide around
the corner of the soundproofed door, thinking no one
could see him. Like a little kid throwing his toys on the
floor and then waiting to see if Mommy will pick them
up, he crouched in a corner to hear what their reaction
would be to his threats! *What an idiot*, thought
Deborah; no low self-esteem there! She thought back
to her conversation with Lizzie and felt more
convinced than ever that self-esteem, like everything
else, is made of thought. Once I think those thoughts

are fact, then I will fall for the lie every time!

Deborah looked out at the runway, watching the planes taxiing and taking off, and she remembered how Shelly had asked her if she was willing to let go of her story when they first met. She suddenly realised that she had always thought that Shelly meant for her to stop retelling it to herself, to drop the narrative of it because it was like torturing herself to continually poke at the wound, holding herself back in the past and never letting it heal. But she suddenly saw that that was only part of it. What she saw now was that the story was just that – a story, actual made up fiction. No wonder letting go of it was such a threatening idea, it had seemed so real. Yes, it happened, and yes, it hurt, but the painful part, the part that she had continued to keep so close to her heart, was only constructed out of her thoughts *about* what had happened, not what actually happened. Wow! The self-pitying thoughts were a fairy tale, a made up myth that she had tortured herself with. If you think something is real, then you can't let it go. The fear of *Who will I be without this* was too painful. The story had become her identity; without it, she would be lost, and that fear was even greater. And then in London, she had become convinced by the "story" that three violent attacks were conclusive justification for a breakdown, nobody could argue with her on that. Three was proof positive that life was out to get her. But who made that up? Who said Three was the magic number that gives a person permission to give up? She had! She had made that up and then tortured herself by repeatedly counting them! See, the fractured skull, that's One, the mugging, that's Two, and the boy who broke my neck, there's my Three! Now I have permission to give up and go nuts! It's like when they say a cat has nine lives, they don't actually mean exactly nine lives. The cat doesn't actually lie down saying, oh well that's it, I had my nine, what can I do? It's not my fault! They just mean a cat seems to be able to keep getting up again. Thank God she had gotten up again. She looked around in her mind to see where her victim story was now but it wasn't there! She hadn't worked on it to make it go away, it had just...gone away like the kids' bubbles it just burst on its own. It occurred to her that the more she saw her experience for what it was, just spiritual energy flowing through her mind, the story of her being a victim had disappeared into thin air. The basketball had become a bubble all on its own, without her needing to do anything. It had gone because it never actually existed other than in her thoughts, so like a nightmare, it had faded in the light of day!

As she walked through the airport to her gate, she stopped at a bookstore to browse. In a display of new books, she saw the story of Roger Banister, the British athlete who had broken the record for running the 4-minute mile. It was the fiftieth anniversary of his record-breaking triumph of speed and endurance. She picked up a copy and started to read. Doctors and coaches had told him it couldn't be done, but amazingly, within weeks of his record-breaking achievement, other athletes began to do it, too! Before, everyone had believed that a 4-minute mile wasn't possible; they had all believed a story that had held them back from achieving their best, even though they were all clearly capable of it! *Amazing*, thought Deborah. She turned the book over: "*No longer conscious of my movement, I discovered a new unity with nature. I had found a new source of power and beauty, a source I never dreamt existed.*" Deborah had been deeply touched by Sheldon's description of the beautiful, quiet place deep inside, where people learn they can "fly" by just letting go. Roger Banister had found it, too. Like herself, so many of the people she worked with, both in Hollywood and at the Center, had been told they were damaged goods, that they would never be able to get back up again and would need to work on themselves for the rest of their lives or the bogeyman subconscious was going to get them, and that was just the way it was. *Good business plan for the psychiatric profession*, thought Deborah cynically, as she paid for the book. If only they could see the truth, that we can't ever be damaged, if only they could feel the Quiet, they would see the truth of what I've seen, that the past is just a story.

Deborah bought herself a hot chocolate and sat in the cafe near Gate 26, waiting for her flight to LA and watching the multitude of travelers passing by, when her eye was caught by a CNN report on a nearby TV. She wasn't sure at first, but then she realised that she was looking at a familiar face…she couldn't quite… *Oh my gosh*, thought Deborah suddenly, *that's Stephanie!!* She got up and moved closer to the screen so she could hear. She couldn't think why or what Stephanie, her very first client from London, could be doing in the CNN studios in New York. But there she was! Deborah just couldn't believe it! She watched in disbelief, it was something to do with UNICEF.

"And this new report shows some damning statistics about the gap between investing in the poorest children and that of the less deprived?" asked the reporter.

"Yes," replied Stephanie, as calm and confident as you like. "The Annual Report highlights UNICEF's contributions to achieving the MDGs by providing assistance towards improving children's health, expanding access to quality education, and protecting children's rights in more than one hundred and fifty countries and territories, including in places of crisis. The report emphasizes how UNICEF is reorienting its programming to more closely target and meet the rights and needs of the most deprived and marginalized children to achieve greater progress with equity."

The reporter went on, but Deborah couldn't really follow what they were talking about; all she could do was keep repeating, that's Stephanie, OMG, *that's Stephanie!!*

The reporter finally thanked Mrs. Stephanie Duval, Director of Children's Rights at UNICEF, Deborah sat back in her chair in amazement.

Wow! She wiped away the tears that were running down her face as she remembered how lost and hopeless Stephanie was when they first met. How she had refused to let what had happened to her stop her from getting better and moving on. She, herself had been one of those children who needed protecting! Deborah was overcome with gratitude, how amazing it felt to be just a small part of turning someone's painful past around and to see them helping those who are as defenseless and vulnerable as she once was. She thought of all the people she had met who hadn't had it half as tough as Stephanie and were still stuck in the past, holding onto a reality that didn't exist anymore.

She remembered the quote on the last page of *The Missing Link...*

Bless those who
have sinned against you,
For they have lost their way.
Reach out your hand
And help them live a happy day.[1]

Wow!

Acknowledgments

I would first like to thank my dear friend Lauren Weinberg for her incredible dedication and encouragement in helping me to get this book out into the world, her feedback, design ideas, and constant support were wonderful. A big thank you also to Miryam Wasserman for the cover photos, Shari Pilo for all her digital help, Sarah Rosenbaum for her superb editing, and the many friends who read and encouraged me to keep going.

This story would not be possible if not for the amazing support of friends, colleagues, and mentors who have supported me, welcomed me into their homes and hearts, and continue to teach and inspire me with their wisdom and generosity.

Nick, Beryl and Jeff Peters, Kirsten Bechhofer, Scott Anderson, John Travolta, Val Jones, Cindy Kaufman, Shelly Kompel, Sheldon Wolfe, Elisa Rubinstein, Esther and Milton Simon, Marty Fox, Carol and Aaron Banayan, Gitty and Yisrael Uri, Karen and Ben Geiger, everyone at Ohr Eliyahu, Miriam and Ari Wasserman, Eli Schulman, Andy and Herschel Alpert, Shimmy and Malka Pine, Chana, Shaul and the whole Rosenblatt family, Shifra Chesler, Miriam and Moshe Frankel, Aaron and Lila Turner, Julian and Joanna Fraser, Jacqueline Hollows, Dr. Bill Petit, and of course, Mr. Sydney Banks.

Bibliography

Chapter 6. Islington 2
1. Frankl, Viktor E. *Man's Search for Meaning*. Boston: Beacon Press, 2006. p 24
2. Frankl, Viktor E. *Man's Search for Meaning*. Boston: Beacon Press, 2006. p 76
3. Peck, M. Scott. The Road Less Traveled: A New Psychology of Love, Traditional Values, and Spiritual Growth. New York: Simon and Schuster, 1978. p 105

Chapter 7. Shoreditch
1. Frankl, Viktor E. *Man's Search for Meaning*. Boston: Beacon Press, 2006 p 24

Chapter 8. Leicester Square
1. Williamson, Marianne. A Return to Love: Reflections on the Principles of "A Course in Miracles." Rev. ed. London: Thorsons, 1996. p190-191

Chapter 21. Jerusalem
1. Banks, Sydney. *The Missing Link*. Edmonton, Alberta: Lone Pine, 2016. p 49
2. Banks, Sydney. *The Missing Link*. Edmonton, Alberta: Lone Pine, 2016. p 102
3. Banks, Sydney. *The Missing Link*. Edmonton, Alberta: Lone Pine, 2016. p 121

Chapter 24. Venice Beach
1. Banks, Sydney. *The Missing Link*. Edmonton, Alberta: Lone Pine, 2016. p 49

Chapter 25. New York
1. Banks, Sydney. *The Missing Link*. Edmonton, Alberta: Lone Pine, 2016. p 142

Resources

Chana Studley leads workshops in person and online and speaks at conferences all over the world. She is available for coaching, mentoring and intensives. *The Myth of Low Self-Esteem* is her first novel, the second, *A Tale of Two Boys* will be available soon.

You can contact her at
chanastudley.com

Recommended reading:
The Missing Link - Sydney Banks
The Enlightened Gardener - Sydney Banks

Anatomy of an Epidemic - Robert Whitiker
Cracked - James Davies

Three Principles resources:
sydneybanks.org
3PGC.org
www.onethought.com
3pconference.org

32248890R00156

Made in the USA
San Bernardino, CA
12 April 2019